AWAKENING THE GIFT

Book I

The Accounts
of a Pleiadian Traveler

Nakala Akasie

Point of Light Pleiadian Publishing

ISBN: 978-1-942445-04-3
(e) ISBN: 978-1-942445-05-0

Library of Congress Control Number: 2015942196

Printed in the United States of America
10 9 8 7 6 5 4 3 2 1

Cover designer: Marsha Slomowitz
Typographer: Marsha Slomowitz
eBook: Marcia Breece

CONTENTS

ACKNOWLEDGEMENTS

When there is Love there is Light.
Tranquil is the Presence of the Lord.

As I awaken to the gifts of God I have found myself in a land of abundance—joy—great wealth that cannot be measured by worldly instruments. My moments here are short, fleeting as grand opportunities for spiritual growth are designed and presented to me of which I know not their true worth. If only I might use them to be pleasing unto Him.

This place we call the Earth, is a fantastic theatre where we take on another identity just like the actor does when he plays his part—his role in an elaborate production. We are all playing our parts to discriminate age defying lessons on honor, truth, and wisdom taking us higher into the field of Light.

*

INTRODUCTION

By Quem Akasie

As one of the co-authors of this work, *Awakening: The Gift,* I wish to make it known that during the writing of this book there were several groups of spiritual guides in addition to the Ascended Masters and Archangels who came to assist Nakala. Always it has been our intention that those personal interactions and teachings be included in this book. I thank all of those who worked on this project, bringing it into the physical reality.

This book is the compilation of Nakala's daily communications and experiences with those of the angelic realm in addition to those on the Earth plane. *Awakening: The Gift* is a true affidavit of a personal transformation.

—Quem

PART
ONE

CHOICES

CHAPTER
ONE

As it happened, I was in the kitchen doing the last minute cleanup from breakfast before heading out the door to drop off the kids for school when out of the corner of my eye I caught a glimpse of dark reddish-brown streaks on the inside of my eldest son's wrists. *Were they cuts?*

Three days remained of school and we had all been looking forward to watching movies late at night, sleeping in, going swimming, and camping out in the mountains. But life, as I have learned, has a way of shifting on a moment's notice right before you reach that place that you really want to be.

A day earlier I had received a phone call from the junior high school counselor, Mr. Higgens, who had earned a reputation for not being the most understanding and kind person. How he had gotten the job as a school counselor I had always wondered. He informed me that we had an unpleasant state of affairs concerning my eldest son and of the consequences thereof. Mr. Higgens had been abrupt, his manner void of compassion as he had driven his point home, "Bradley's grades are unacceptable and therefore he must be enrolled in summer school before he will permitted to pass to the next grade." He had paused momentarily before adding in a subtle yet condescending tone, "He, of course, will be expected to earn acceptable marks," like I hadn't known that.

Temporarily stunned, I had gently set the receiver down on the cradle. The phone call had left me feeling disappointed. The more I thought about it, I realized that I was angry that our summer months would be disrupted because of my son's choices.

I felt cheated. I had worked outside the home since my youngest son was two years old. I had quit work to stay home with the kids…for reasons that will become apparent as you read.

It was my first summer that I had home with the kids. Even though I had worked outside the home for years, I still had hauled these kids to and from school. I had been looking forward to some down time. I wanted a rest from it all. It seemed to me that my time off would never arrive. I was angry all right. It had been a good thing the kids had been in school when the call came in because I needed time to sort this through and let the anger dissipate—to make a plan.

After some reflection, I had to admit that part of this was my fault because I had known that Bradley's grades had been slipping for some time. I had seen a steady decline in them every nine-week period to the point that I dreaded when the grade cards came out. I had hoped that Bradley would bring them up before the year had ended.

Yes, I had chided myself; there were the obvious signs that he had just been skating by. Unfortunately, I had only chosen to verbally reprimand him for not keeping on track with his studies and let it go. I should have taken a firmer approach, but I thought that it was a passing phase…I had reasoned it would be better not to push him and let him find his way. So many kids go through times like these, I thought.

Over the school year, I had watched Bradley withdraw—growing temperamental—more sullen. I hadn't known what to attribute his mood or his behavior to.

With little or no provocation, Bradley would swiftly fly into a belligerent rage that was often directed toward his two younger siblings. I swallowed hard as I recounted the times when I had not been able to protect my children from their brother's abusive outbursts. I had decided to quit my job so I could watch over them more closely.

I reprimanded myself saying that I would no longer allow myself to turn a blind eye. Something was troubling Bradley. It was time to face it…past time to face it, even though I didn't know what I was facing.

The evening of the phone call from Mr. Higgens, I had approached Bradley and had candidly laid out the facts as I knew them. There wasn't all that much to it. He had failed two classes and had to make them up. He had to attend summer school. End of story. We talked about some real consequences to his actions but hadn't come to any solutions that felt comfortable. So we had left it all up in the air. Bradley had not had any solid punishment or direction given to him. Perhaps summer school was punishment enough.

For months, I had felt that, as a family, we had been walking on something akin to a rocky crag or precipice. The edge had been sharp, jagged, and precarious. In places the rocks were beginning to break free—separating from the other rocks and falling, hitting, and breaking as they traveled downward out of control. I had compared my entire family to the rocks: if we shifted in any one direction a little too much we might easily lose our balance and fall, breaking into a thousand pieces before any of us could find a way to stop the momentum.

The entire year, we had struggled to maintain peace by what I had thought had been clever at the time: we simply headed off any angry outbursts by redirecting the subject to something more pleasant. This meant we had to be alert at all times and extra careful around Bradley. We hadn't wanted to upset him. However, the probability had been strong that sooner or later we would make a wrong choice, sending him into a rage that couldn't be turned back. Our lives, like the rough rocks that had loosened, would have nothing left to hang onto—to brace us from the fall.

My children, all of them, had suffered somewhat from my lack of attention concerning Bradley's schooling as most of my concentration had been centered on keeping peace in the household instead of on his grades…on what was troubling him.

My thoughts suddenly took a front seat to how much of my energy would be used to see that Bradley got to and from summer school and making sure he completed his assignments. Long gone were the dreams of a leisurely summer.

Well, I shook my head in defiance, there is nothing I can do to change this unfortunate set of circumstances. I figured it would be best to focus on the free time we, as a family, had left of summer instead of what glared in our faces: summer school.

As I made peace with the situation I dug deeper. The grades along with his attitude had merely been signs, a symptom of something that was disturbing him. *What could have been that awful?*

Not only had Bradley not applied himself in school, but also his actions had become reckless—his choices were dangerous, against the law, and life threatening.

A few weeks earlier, I had had the misfortune of playing hostess to the sheriff and then a few days later to the two representatives of the Santa Fe Railroad, which ran near our home. It seemed Bradley had gotten himself into trouble. There was an investigation being conducted. I listened and had pondered my choices, weighing them all carefully.

Thinking Bradley needed someone to confide in and direction, I decided to take him to see a therapist. He certainly wouldn't talk to me or to his father about what he had gotten into. *What was the root of his agitation?*

After what I had thought had been a thorough evaluation by the therapist, it was recommended that Bradley see a colleague, a psychiatrist, Dr. Greene for another evaluation for ADD (attention deficit disorder). Then Dr. Greene promptly convinced me that the desired action would be to put him on medication.

Bradley, then fourteen, was enrolled in the eighth grade. My two younger children were both attending the grade school. The day after the phone call—the day after I had talked to Bradley about the repercussions of his behavior was the same day that I caught a glimpse of the inside of his wrists—the streaks of dark red.

My voice, with suspicion and dread, rose to a pitch I didn't readily recognize. I faced Bradley and commanded him to turn his wrists over so I could get a better look. My mind went into hyper drive. *What had happened? Did he require medical attention?*

Without resistance, Bradley complied, as if nothing was wrong. There were several cuts on the inside of each wrist that were razor thin. The cuts were deep enough to have bled and scabbed over, but had not been life threatening. I was flabbergasted—afraid of what this meant, and I lost my composure.

Pointedly, I asked him what had happened. Bradley's reason for the injury was flimsy, having no merit whatsoever. Void of emotion, Bradley's response was that he had been on the roof of our ranch-style home and as he climbed down he had slid down over the gutter. I didn't buy his story. *What had he been doing on the roof anyway? I didn't believe him.*

Without hesitation, I reached for the phone and dialed the emergency number for the therapist only to have the answering service pick up. Distraught and desperate, I left my message, concerned that critical hours might pass by before he would get back to me. However, in less than five minutes the therapist returned my call.

Somewhat relieved that I had someone with expertise to confide in, I told him what I had seen and repeated my conversation that I had had with my son. "Of course, I will see to his care," the therapist assured me before adding, "However, Dr. Greene should know what is going on. I am sure Dr. Greene will want to admit Bradley so we can watch over him properly. I will notify the doctor immediately." *Admit him?* With his words he had intended to relieve my apprehension; instead though, I felt the anxiety quicken and build. My heart grew heavy as I heard myself agree to his recommendation.

That morning marked the beginning of the end as my son was admitted to the hospital for a mental assessment and observation. In hind-sight, I know now that this action had weighed heavily on my son, creating feelings of doubt, being unloved, not being good enough, not being under-stood. In essence it had created a stigma that would weigh heavily on my son for the rest of his short life. The emotions had been palpable. Bradley no longer trusted us. He no longer trusted anyone.

Searching for clues for how I could best talk to my son to assure him that we wanted him safe, I read his body language and studied his facial expressions. All I saw was contempt and anger. He had slammed the door shut and locked it. His clear, unmistakable, though unspoken message had been, "I am not interested in talking…to any of you!"

In retrospect, I am able to see it clearly. It was as if we had been writing a book—Bradley's book—and this was the very last chapter. I could see that each person in his life—his brother and sister, teachers, therapists, police, emergency medical technicians, doctors, nurses, family members, friends, kids on the school bus, our neighbors, and even his dog, Kurt—had been characters in his drama!

The thing was, the plot had been written by Brad's actions, or reactions, to what other people had said or done to him. The narrative had been written moment by moment with each thought, feeling, and action in response to what other people did. Some of the choices people made had made a direct impact on Bradley's decisions; others had not. The main character, Bradley, had full control—the final say on how the plot evolved and the story ended.

I saw how even one phone call had made a huge impact on Bradley's life and how it had created a snow ball effect that led to a series of unfortunate choices—choices that no one could change, not ever. *But really, why had Bradley been so angry? Why did he do these things that were so dangerous?*

As parents we had a certain amount of control, or so it had seemed. Perhaps that was what Bradley wanted to show us. we were not in control. He was not to be controlled!

As I looked at the situation more closely, I saw that everyone I knew had tried to support Bradley. He had been in a rough patch for sure. Everyone concerned had been following Bradley's lead. We all were involved and in a way, somewhat responsible for what had happened.

All the players had waited for their cues. According to the actors' beliefs and how well they controlled their thoughts, emotions, and actions, they had contributed drama…substance to the story. Most all who were playing their parts in the delicate but paramount scene had been doing so unconsciously: not aware of how important their interactions were with Bradley and the decisions they made concerning him.

Unfortunately, as if on auto-pilot, many of the people who had influenced the outcome of this particular scene in Brad's life (Brad's choices) were teachers and doctors who work with scores of people each year, many of whom were working from a text-book mentality and not from their hearts.

In other words, the choices were made without looking closely at the entire picture: Bradley's feelings. Some of the choices had been irreversible, having such a massive impact on how the scheme of it all played out.

Many of us were left exposed and vulnerable and to a larger degree, as a result of the choices made, were shattered…unable to escape the nuances of life's greater mysteries: life and death.

There seemed to be no sure way to finish this chapter of Bradley's book or for any of us to walk away a winner or even minutely unscathed from life's theater, as we all had been locked into the drama as we set about making our own choices. As sure as the sun rises and sets, by his own volition, he made his choice and he himself wrote the last line.

For the main character, Bradley, there was no account taken to how we, the supporting actors, would follow his lead as he wrote his thoughts and feelings down on the pages with color and flare in one irrefutable gesture like he had literally taken his hand and swept it before us to banish us all out of his way—out of his sight. His thoughts were intrinsically fueled by fear, anger, and hate that ultimately dominated. He wanted to remove us from his story. *Or was it the other way around? Had he wanted to remove himself?*

No matter how many times I replayed the scenario of Bradley's last days I was not able to make sense of it all.

* * *

After the tedious affair of the funeral service, hearing each person offer their sincere condolences, and seeing to the final effort of laying his body to rest, I began to grieve in silence. I didn't want anyone, especially my children, to see me scream, or cry, or cling to my husband for dear life.

The loss of my son left me in absolute torment. In secrecy, as if I were replaying a TV broadcast over and over, and unmercifully, I saw the last week of his life leading up to his "death" over and over. I was unable to shut down the images, the thoughts, the emotions, or my incessant questions. The scene continued to present itself over and over as if it were the very first time—fresh, alive, and absolute—holding my mind in torment every moment of each day and night. Never did the episode change.

I was unable to sleep, so I called my doctor asking for sleeping pills. Even they did not ease the agony or facilitate a single restful night's sleep.

My tears spilled over, my eyes burned, my throat was raw, and my head ached. Mentally, emotionally, and physically I was spent. I was no longer the same person. Yet outwardly, I persevered, taking charge of my family and continuing to fulfill my duties as a mother, wife, and homemaker.

Inwardly, I ached. My family was no longer complete, intact. My eldest child was gone, leaving a huge, gaping hole in my life. Everything I saw reminded me of Bradley: his room, the TV, the school, school buses, the hospital, the church, cemeteries, grocery shopping, cooking, even setting the dinner table—triggered me—evoking emotions that I wished never to feel again. So I pushed past it all and pretended I didn't see or feel, hoping that it all would just disappear and release me from reliving the pain.

For weeks people offered their support with sympathetic gestures by sending cards and flowers, speaking thoughtful words…*What did they know? How could they know? I knew they just wanted to be kind, but why did they insist on reminding me of it? I wanted to forget!* Superficially, I smiled and thanked them. Secretly, I grew frustrated and angry that I had yet again been reminded of my pain, my son who was gone…forever.

Going into deep introspection, I began to ask questions, hoping to find the answers that would somehow ease my mind…fill my heart with comfort and peace. Over and over, I relived every word, every scenario, working to find the magic answer to what had gone wrong.

My thoughts drifted back time and time again to a sermon I had heard as a young girl. The Baptist preacher had been quite charismatic and persuasive, driving his point in deep during one of his sermons classifying suicide as the ultimate sin. He had stated with such profound authority that if a person ended his or her life, they would be cast into the fiery depths of hell. The scene had been deeply embedded into my young impressionable mind.

Why had Bradley chosen that path? What if I had done something different? If only I listened more closely. If only I had asked more questions.

Then other questions came. *What had happened to the soul who had inhabited that body? Where had it gone? Did he vanish into thin air? Had he gone to hell like the preacher had stated? Is someone (a relative perhaps) looking after him in the spirit world? Exactly what had happened to him?*

No matter how many questions I came up with, I refused to believe that Bradley had gone to this place of torment or simply had vanished—that he no longer existed on any level.

I was his mother, after all, and I wanted—no—*needed* peace of mind that he was somewhere safe and being attended to.

CHAPTER
TWO

Years passed and with it my children grew and moved out to be on their own and with the extra time came an intense period of study. I immersed myself in subjects of the metaphysical—the spiritual—life after death. I had found from my research that there was a missing link in my understanding—a piece of crucial information had been disregarded—glossed over. We are eternal Beings of Light who have taken embodiment in the flesh (incarnated) repeatedly. Without this knowledge how could anyone understand what happens to the soul when the physical body perishes?

Previously, I had no knowledge of this information. None of the institutions, schools, or churches that I had attended had taught this crucial yet basic truth. In my mid-western town this pivotal information had somehow been forgotten.

Attaining this core piece of information generated a deeper understanding that we *are* spiritual beings. We come to this realm to learn God's truths—to be the expressions of the Divine in the physical realm.

PART
TWO

PENDULUMS:
WHAT ARE THEY FOR?

CHAPTER
THREE

Several years later, after many spiritual books studied, classes and events attended…I received a phone call late one afternoon from a friend, Beth, inviting me to join her on an impromptu jaunt to Garnett, Kansas.

We had met at the County Extension Master Gardener organization and had become fast friends. Beth was a bit older and into metaphysics and I found that our conversations about spirit were stimulating.

The purpose of the trip to Garnett was to check out some energy in an old, brick building. To be clear, when I say "check out," I mean we went to feel the energy and to see if we might be able to understand a deeper meaning or to identify its source.

Being familiar with the building, I remembered it was one of the oldest buildings on the city square and was currently used as a storefront for antiques. The building was a very deep, two-story brick building with a basement.

Donna, the current owner of the business, was seeking confirmation from outside sources concerning some odd activity that she had been experiencing in her store. At that time I was unaware that Donna regularly used a pendulum to receive information.

With the town of Garnett being located approximately sixty miles south of where we lived, I could easily surmise that we had very little time to make the drive *and* get some dinner. After some discussion, Beth and I agreed to meet at her place, drive to Garnett in her vehicle, grab a fast bite, and then head over to the site.

Directly after we arrived, pleasantries were exchanged; and Beth and I immediately headed upstairs to explore. The second floor had a drop ceiling and was being used to display all sorts of merchandise from several different vendors. Because dealers used shelving units, makeshift walls, and even large pieces of furniture to set their merchandise apart, our view of the entire floor was somewhat obstructed.

Not long after we arrived, I found myself standing alone among the mix of wares displayed in every nook and cranny. I remember feeling a little discombobulated, so for a little reassurance I moved out into one of the larger isles to get a better view of the large room: I wanted to see Beth. For some reason I just felt better if she were within eyesight. I scanned the room and quickly found her, so my tension diminished somewhat.

For a moment, I just stood there and reminded myself why I was there. Then intentionally, I set my focus, making mental notes on which part of the room I felt any shifts in energy. Also, I paid careful attention to the vibrational shifts in my physical body *and* what thoughts and emotions arose during each assessment. As I walked the perimeter of the upstairs floor, I mentally sectioned off the room in blocks, connecting to what energy I felt in certain areas, near specific objects, and pieces of furniture.

There was one area in particular with extremely high energy that I connected with for several minutes. The energy was located in an individual's booth along the outer brick wall. There were no windows on that particular wall, just the white-washed brick with nothing special that I could detect that might emanate a higher frequency associated with the articles in the booth—just glassware, doilies, antique baby clothing and so on. Nothing there was unusual in the least that might emit a high charge of energy. Finding the area in question expansive, I spent several minutes scanning the wall to measure any fluctuations and to see just how large the area was. I also felt how far away from the wall the energy extended. I noticed the fluorescent light above, listened to its hum, and wondered how much of its energy interfered or complemented the energy that seemed to radiate from the wall itself. Not coming to any clear conclusions, I decided to move on.

Soon Beth and I regrouped near an area where a hardwood bedroom set was being displayed that I calculated to be about fifty to seventy years old. I noted that the furniture was situated near the stairwell; and as I lingered there, the feelings of sadness and pain—even a sense of abandonment—unexpectedly arose, becoming more intense the longer I remained.

In a matter of fact way, I stated to Beth what I felt while I stood in that specific area. I didn't know if the feelings were associated with the furniture or not, but they seemed to be as I had walked away from the furniture several times and back to test what I was feeling. Beth and I agreed it was quite odd to feel those emotions. Deciding it was time to explore another floor we headed for the stairs.

As we descended the two flights going down into the basement, instantly I felt the drop in temperature several degrees and the smell of *old* overtook. Uncomfortable memories surfaced of the last time I had been there in that same basement on an outing with a couple of friends.

There had been three of us taking a girls' day out. One of the women, who incidentally was of the Lakota Tribe, (American Indian) had the gift of sight (the ability to see spirits) and had walked a few feet away from us and had turned to step around a dividing wall out of our sight. Suddenly, I heard her shriek. Thinking she had hurt herself, I had rushed to her side to assist her only to find that she had not been injured at all. Since she was obviously dazed, I waited for her to calm herself. She had explained that as she had gone around the corner she had almost walked into an Indian warrior who had been standing there poised with his arms across his chest. Personally, I had never seen anything like that down there myself but had felt the overwhelming impression that the basement was just plain creepy. My opinion had been and still was that I would just as soon avoid the place all together.

With a sufficient amount of effort, I set aside those recollections. However, I wasn't able to set aside the dark foreboding feeling. To put it bluntly, I wanted out of there as quickly as I could, but for appearances sake I outwardly presented myself as aloof and unconcerned. To enable me to continue my research, I used a mind game—the tactic that I was on a grand expedition: I might find something fetching or quite possibly of high value hiding among the many articles that had gathered dust and cobwebs.

The basement didn't seem to be as large as the other floors. There were walls built here and there; and because of inadequate lighting, there were dark, foreboding shadows cast in various places. I found the corners were even darker and more ominous and I avoided them all together. In general, the basement was dark and gloomy with a dank, musty smell creating the final component to make the ambiance of a haunted building complete.

Most of the larger pieces that were for sale, such as large steamer trunks, mirrors, farm equipment and gates for fences, were displayed down there and were for us uninteresting. Not wanting to tarry, we made our way around the floor with as much speed and accuracy as we could muster.

The upstairs and the basement were the floors with stagnant energy, pools of emotional energy and trauma, and areas with noticeable shifts in the vibrations. Beth and I both had identified areas with much higher energy patterns in some places that Donna later confirmed.

After we had walked the entire basement (minus the corners) we agreed it was time to call it quits, head back to the main floor, and meet as a group to discuss our findings. Donna motioned for us to have a seat on a ten-foot walnut-stained oak church pew with hand-carved, decorative arms and legs in her makeshift office, then offered us some hot ginger-lemon tea and sugar cookies. At one point during our discussion, Donna reached into her pocket and pulled out a pendulum. As we talked about different areas of the building where we had sensed different energy patterns, higher frequencies, and foreboding feelings, she held up the pendulum and it swung in circles. Being a little familiar with dowsing, I speculated that she was connecting with some sort of energy, but still I thought it weird.

When I spoke of the emotions I felt near the bedroom furniture, Donna disclosed there had been a fire upstairs that had taken the life of a young girl. She also spoke about various spirits that hung around, a possible star gate or portal along the white brick wall, space travelers, and hidden treasure in the basement. Of course there had been the issue of emotional attachments being on pieces of furniture and treasured items.

As the conversation neared its close, Donna casually mentioned that we may be interested in a two-day seminar that was being put together impromptu. She pulled out the flier and held it out for Beth to take. I scooted closer to Beth as she held out the sheet so I could read it along with her. The title read, *Advanced Dowsing: Healing & Self-Empowerment Seminar*. Mid-way down the paper I read the long list of topics that would be covered in the class, like how to reduce stress, find a way to collect money from someone who owes it to you, overcome fear, reach a realm of the Spirit World, and Meet your Spirit Guides, just to name a few. Strangely the words, *Meet your Spirit Guides* seemed to rise off the page.

Donna continued her sales pitch by stating the seminar had been organized by a couple of local women who were evidentially highly impressed with the presenter. Raymon, the presenter, was from the hills of West Virginia and would be in the area and available to teach his seminar before he traveled back home to the east.

The information on the brochure seemed impressive *and* conclusive. The entry for meeting your spirit guides definitely sparked my interest to the point that I felt that I had seen just enough to hook me.

Understanding energy is a powerful force—we both felt it was always best to be open-minded about anything concerning energy. In other words, we had learned not to discount anything as there are unseen forces at hand that we, as humans, know little to nothing of. We both were intensely intrigued with the mystery of it all and the possibilities that communicating with our guides might present!

I glanced at Beth and gave her an affirmative nod indicating that I was in. She smiled and returned the nod. There was no need for us to go home and *think* about our options. Right then, I said to Donna, "We want to take the seminar. How do we sign up?"

Just as I said the words 'sign up', I saw the date and where it would be taking place. The seminar was in four days in southern Missouri! A feeling of uncertainty overtook. *Could we ready ourselves that quickly?* We both had responsibilities to see to before we would be able to leave town. I reviewed the particulars again, wondering if this was such a great idea after all. *What was it that I required to do to get ready for this trip? How long would it take me?* I calculated my list, surmising that I could be ready in time. Could Beth?

The workshop was scheduled to take place in Bradleyville, Missouri. When I saw the name, Bradleyville, on the brochure, I about choked.

Instead, though, I managed to suck in a breath as I felt my heart skip a beat. I looked away hoping that no one had noticed my reaction. Bradleyville, of all the names of towns to be—why did it have to be this one? Bradleyville had triggered unsettling memories of my son. I swallowed hard and reminded myself that Bradleyville was just a name. I looked away as I worked to I dismiss my feelings of discomfort and grief.

On the map I found Bradleyville to be located pretty much in the central-southern portion of Missouri. For us, who were from northeastern Kansas, this would not be a fast drive, by any means. Anyone who has driven in southern Missouri and into Arkansas would be well aware the roads are notoriously two-lane, snaking up, around, and down steep mountain grades. If you happened to get stuck behind a slower vehicle, it might be a long, tedious stretch before you had an opportunity to pass. Undoubtedly, the other fact seasoned travelers were well aware of is the further south one travels in rural areas, the less likely it is to find facilities (restrooms). Simply put, Bradleyville was in the middle of nowhere.

The seminar, Donna, as our new friend, explained to us, would be in The Meeting Room at the Getaway Gift Shop located at the intersection of highways 125 and 76. She said, "You will see the gas station on the right." Adding, "It is the only building there. The little store where we will meet shares occupancy with the gas station. Bradleyville is a very small place—just a little spot on the side of the road." Then she closed with the over-used adage, "If you blink you will miss it."

Donna ruminated a bit before elaborating, "Currently there is a problem with the plumbing. We may have to walk next door to use the gas station's rest room." She continued on with, "There are no nearby places for a sit-down meal, so the locals will be preparing lunch for everyone. There are the typical vending machines at the gas station." Inwardly, I groaned at the implications. Beth and I exchanged a knowing glance to one another, signaling that we were clear that there might be some unpleasant bumps; but our sense of adventure had kicked into high gear. We both knew that we wanted to make the trip.

Naturally, since Beth and I had traveled a fair amount in the southern part of Missouri, we had been preconditioned about how things worked *down there.* Simply said, there were areas that were better equipped than others. As women, naturally, some of our main concerns were food and *clean* toilet facilities.

Nevertheless, we were extremely grateful to have been given this opportunity to take the weekend workshop and willing to travel the distance to take a chance that there might not be a great place to eat or to do our business. We decided we could pack a large cooler full of food. At least this would cover part of our concerns.

I noted that as soon as Donna explained a little more about the seminar, it was as if something deep inside of me had been switched on—a surge of adrenalin perhaps? A really powerful force had caused me to take notice, pulling me in; I knew I had to be there.

What I planned to do, where I planned to go defied all practical logic. It didn't matter, though. Promptly, I assessed my duties as a wife. Surely my husband could easily take care of the place and the cat for a few days in my absence.

The next few days presented themselves in a flurry. I found myself skillfully packing my bags, withdrawing money from my bank account, and filling my car with gas to go on this road trip…to do what? Learn to communicate with my spirit guides. Even though communicating with my spirit guides sounded a bit on the crazy side, I shrugged my shoulders and surrendered to the notion. I knew how I felt: deep inside there was a desire that was so strong that any logical thinking that surfaced was instantly disregarded.

Once we arrived safely at our destination, The Meeting Room, in Bradleyville, we saw that a fairly large group had already gathered. Remarkably, we found that no one had been given any longer than ten days notification to prepare and make the trip. We were pleasantly relieved to find that all of the plumbing concerns had been corrected before we arrived and that there were restaurants and overnight accommodations a mere ten to fifteen minutes away.

I saw that the medium-sized room was nearly full; and at the back stood an older gentleman of medium stature wearing faded blue jeans, a plaid shirt complete with a bolo tie, cowboy boots, and a straw cowboy hat, holding a pendulum. *Is that what he is going to use?* Beth and I stole a glance at one another. *Is that him?*

As I scanned the room, I saw that many of the people were already seated with handouts and pendulums lying on the tables in front of them. I made a mental note that neither of us had a pendulum nor I had never used one. But as I turned around to see where the booklets were, I saw that they had set up a table to display and sell some of their merchandise (pendulums) for the class.

Quickly Beth and I each purchased a pendulum, picked up our information packets, and chose a nearby table to sit at.

As soon as Raymon was satisfied that everyone had arrived, found their seats, and had gotten comfortable, he began his presentation, alternating between three different dowsing tools: a pendulum, rods, and another item that looked like a metal spiral top. (I had never seen one like it before or since.)

In our packets we had received a list of questions to ask using our pendulum. Holding our pendulums in the proper position we obediently followed Raymon down the list.

I noticed that some of the people sitting nearby were having difficulty with their pendulums. In many cases the pendulums did not move or would just slightly wiggle. With each question, my pendulum, however, would respond with such a force, I wondered what to attribute the difference to.

CHAPTER
FOUR

The dowsing seminar proved to be educational as well as entertaining. The class-time went by swiftly and the instructor, Raymon, introduced and managed to cover an extensive amount of background material in order that we would be ready to begin our practice of dowsing on our own.

What is dowsing? Dowsing is an ancient art of finding natural resources such as water, oil, minerals, and/or lost objects. But in Raymon's seminar we learned that dowsing could be used for so much more. We learned to release and transmute energy, measure energy, do healing work, and also connect to the unseen realms to answer our questions.

When Raymon asked his question using his pendulum, he received the answer through the pendulum from his spiritual guides. The answer was denoted by how the pendulum or device would swing, spin, or move.

The weekend flew by and before we knew it the class had ended. We were ready to go home.

After we had driven home from the seminar, I enthusiastically began to practice communicating with my guides using my pendulum. At first, I asked simple questions. Then the questions grew more complex. It was then that I began to notice a real inconsistency with the answers I was getting. Logically, I knew there was a reason for the irregularity, but I wasn't able to figure out what it was; so I bought a notebook and began to document my communications with them. Even then, I wasn't able to establish the real cause for the discrepancies, but I did not stop my work with the pendulum.

Not much time had passed before I saw a real shift in my behavior. I had become more and more obsessed with my practices with the pendulum to learn more about different subjects.

During my entire life I had never considered myself to be obsessive in nature. However, with this new way of communication, that is all I wanted to do! I was so excited to connect and learn about my guides, the higher realms, and even those who had passed on from this Earth that I managed to use all of my free time for that purpose. With the pendulum I felt that I could ask any question and receive the answer almost instantly. I also worked to learn about negative and positive energies and how to transmute the lower energies into Light.

After just two incredible days in Missouri, my life had radically shifted. I was primarily focused on different areas I wanted to learn about. Because of my insatiable desire to know, the pendulum was securely tucked into my pocket so I could easily grab it in a moment's notice.

Quite honestly, I did not want to do much of anything else. However, I continued to do my household chores and everything else that I had always done. When my husband was home, I saw myself secretly steal moments by walking out of his sight to ask my guides questions.

In the evenings after my husband came home from work, I would serve a nice meal, quickly clean up the dishes and spend a little "quality" time with him by watching a TV show and maybe having some dessert. Then I'd politely excuse myself and go upstairs to work.

Earlier on in the year, I began to develop a predictable routine in the evenings. For me, there was no longer any desire to sit in front of the TV with my husband. Instead, I wanted time for personal enrichment, which included listening to music, reading spiritual material, meditating, and journaling.

I thought my husband was fine with me doing my own thing. He had, after all, the TV to entertain him.

Recently, I had just expanded my routine by adding some time to practice automatic writing (channeled writing). These practices assisted in opening up my third eye and I began to receive visions as well.

For me, it was straightforward: I'd *do* my time with my husband then go and have *my alone* time. My evenings were packed to the hilt with stuff I loved to do. However, I saw there was a definite downside. I felt so acutely uncomfortable and even on edge by my actions. I was not only pulling away from my family, my husband, my friends, and I didn't even have a good excuse for doing so! I felt like I was going against what was expected of me, and then I felt guilty for doing so!

No longer had I any desire to spend time visiting with people who talked about mundane subjects. Those times became literally painful as I listened to dramas being created before me. I began to easily recognize when anyone went into judgment concerning others. Even though I loved these people, for me it had become too distressing to be in their company. I had mixed emotions concerning this. I saw what was in the making. I had transitioned into a period of seclusion to connect with the unseen.

Part of me felt ashamed as if I was cheating on my husband—not living up to my commitment. I didn't openly talk about what I did when I retreated in the evenings. As I look back I can discern that I had been hiding because I felt he wouldn't approve of my activities. In truth, I felt what I was doing would be considered wrong. In addition, I felt guilty because I had been intentionally keeping secrets.

With the pendulum, in an almost an obsessive state, I had worked to establish a relationship with my spiritual guides. It seemed I had a million questions to ask them. I asked about life after death—my past lives. I asked about Bradley and other relatives who had passed on. I asked questions about people who were living. The questions were endless! As I continued to ask questions, I continued to get answers that just didn't jibe. What was happening here? I just couldn't seem to get a handle on why this was happening. As time continued, the anxiety began to build.

PART
THREE

THEN THEY CAME
SPIRIT GUIDES AND THE LIKE

CHAPTER
FIVE

Then one night, no different than any other, I was upstairs work-ing with my pendulum when someone unexpectedly began to communicate with me in another way besides answering me with the pendulum.

To this day I have no conscious memory of when or how the actual communications began. But at some point I began to hear words internally or telepathically—someone was talking to me and answering my questions.

I strongly advise anyone who intends to use any sort of divination tool to set the intention of communicating only with the Divine Ones, the Spirit Guides. Saying a short prayer to ask for Divine guidance and protection is the correct protocol when you work with beings in higher realms. When you say a prayer, do it with the feelings of love and grati-tude. For instance, say, "I am grateful that I have the Highest Most Divine Creative Awareness assisting and protecting me always. What I receive is for the highest good of all creation."

Also, it is advisable to have a mentor available to assist you when you are learning to use a pendulum and to communicate with your guides. Many times a mentor may not be available; this is part of the reason these books are being written.

As a novice, I presumed I had one or two guides that might communi-cate with me using the pendulum. As a novice, I had not set any intentions or affirmations to communicate only with my Divine guidance. As a novice, it didn't even occur to me to say a prayer of protection.

After a two-day seminar I thought that I knew exactly how to communicate. Never did I suspect that I would encounter such a challenge. I just *assumed* I'd get my spirit guide. In addition, I did not personally know anyone who knew about pendulums and how to use them properly.

After a lot of soul searching and living in fear of communicating with some sort of evil entity, finally I decided to open up to Beth about my experience. I felt so afraid to reveal what was happening, but after a while I just couldn't hold it in any longer.

At first, she held her tongue, not saying anything. Then she made it clear that she had not had the same experience as me nor had she any knowledge about this sort of thing happening to anyone else. Hence she was very guarded and apprehensive with what little I had told her. After some thought, her recommendation to me was to stop using the pendulum and to stop talking to the *voices*.

Somehow, I had opened up a gateway that allowed a different kind of communication to take place. I began to receive communications with several beings that said they were not my spirit guides. *Who exactly were these guys?* Not understanding the different levels of energy beings, I felt concerned and skeptical; and fear began to take a front seat in my life. However, I kept going forward!

I had been so excited to communicate with my guides that I failed to use discernment, and now I understand that I didn't fully understand how to phrase my questions properly. When a question is asked, it must be specific. Questions are always answered in the present tense, unless otherwise specified, and are answered yes or no.

Fortunately, at the workshop I had acquired a circular chart with letters, enabling me to get answers like the names of my guides and full sentences if I chose to.

Since that time, it has been explained to me that we, individually and as a mass consciousness, are constantly changing our reality according to where we put our intention (our choices that we make), so working on future events, for me, was not something that was encouraged. To quote the Beings of Light, "There are possibilities and probabilities. Very little is absolute in the world of form."

This has been just a very quick overview. Right now I am not going explain in detail the proper way to pose a question to any Being of Light. Just know that there is a proper way.

Because I had been creating open-ended questions I received answers that contradicted themselves. I might ask the same question in exactly the same manner five times and get three of the answers as a yes and two of the answers a no. Well, if this sort of thing happens, if one is not the wiser, it can promote a bit of anxiety and fear. Negative, as well as positive emotions are very powerful.

I have hesitated to reveal my entire story because quite frankly, what I did shows the depth of my naivety. I brought all the confusion upon myself, and some of it I consider to be quite embarrassing; but I will tell my story because I know that I am not the only one in this world who could use a good lesson on discernment.

PART
FOUR

MASTER QUEM
FROM PLEIADES SPEAKS

CHAPTER
SIX

As part of Quem's introduction to me he said, "Long ago, the ancient Akasie (pronounced Ä-kä-sē) gifted me with my name, Quem (pronounced Kwöm). My name simply means to venture forth and to begin anew. I am one of the many Akasie leaders, master teachers, and guides from Pleiades, who give forth teachings through the written word. I am your Master Guide and Pleiadian father.

"Many years have passed since the time when I ventured forth with thousands of other members from our star system. We became as *ONE* to give forth our services to all of those of your great planet. Our intention has been clearly stated: We have pledged our lives to be of assistance to the many and diverse peoples of the Earth plane.

"In addition, to those from Pleiades, there are a great many other benevolent beings who represent numerous star nations who have also chosen to join in this great cause.

"We have all traveled far from our homelands to forge beautiful and lasting friendships benefiting all of creation. Together, we have built a solid foundation pledging that we, as a whole, will always be united in one cause, always giving of ourselves to all peoples, in all places, and in all ways that promote not only peace and harmony but also love. We are a diverse group, but collectively we have joined as One Nation serving God, our Creator.

"As we go forward into the New Age of Aquarius, we strive to serve those of you who walk the Earth plane to your highest good. To you, we offer our alliance, allegiance, knowledge, and wisdom. To you, we offer what we hold most dear to our hearts, which is none other than our own selves. In full faith, we come to you as you remember your true essence of love.

"Always, I, as with all others, wait until the time is nigh when you on the Earth plane ask for guidance from the Ones of the Most High. It is only then that we may assist you by giving the universal teachings.

"So you see, as you continue on your path, there are scores of masters and guides from untold nations who are readily available for you as you make your steps, ever gaining a higher level of understanding. Always, we pray that you will welcome us and allow us to remain by your side as we continue through the evolutionary process.

"In the very first days of our communication, I had instructed you to write down all communications with the beings who come to you. In addition, you were to document all exchanges with family and friends and explore your thoughts and feelings in your journal. In general terms, you were asked to document your life. Openly, I stated we would be writing books for those who reside on Earth.

"This did not come as any surprise to you. Look back, my young daughter, and see the steps that have taken you to bring you to this very moment. The interest for writing has always been there close to the surface ready to break free. You have even taken every college course available to assist you in your writing skills, training you for this very assignment."

Quietly, I retreated into the recesses of my mind as Quem spoke on his disclosure concerning the books. I recognized that they were like puzzle pieces or steps that I had to take in order to get where I am and they were finally coming together, fitting together perfectly. I felt my vibration swell with gratitude and love. It all made perfect sense! The words, 'We are going to write a book together' had blazed through me like a brilliant all-consuming light, yet it had been soft like a sweet embrace. The energy behind the words had evoked something familiar and dear and had fulfilled my every unspoken desire. At last I saw that my life had taken flight, gaining new meaning and purpose. I had always wanted to write.

"Yes," Quem revealed, "I had told you that the name of our first book would be, *When Angels Speak*. That book is now completed and printed and continues to serve as a great teaching tool. It also serves untold nations as through your process of getting down information (memories and teachings), this promoted a great source of healing. As you wrote you explored and uncovered many of life's mysteries that have held you captive and imprisoned for eons.

"Through the writing process you were freed—released from bondage. With your liberation there follows the liberation of countless others! (You set into motion the energy of healing for the body of the masses. It continues on!) In addition, you satisfied nearly all of your karmic debt in the writing of *When Angels Speak!*

"I am pleased to hold the title of Master Writer for this book, our first book in *The Accounts of a Pleiadian Traveler*, as I am master contributor, or writer, of this work. However, I am not the only person who is assisting in this work. In addition, there are many others—my brothers and sisters—the Akasie from the Pleiades who sit in council bringing forth great creative sparks of illumination—ideas—concerning any enduring enterprise and therefore are assisting in the endeavor. We have many more books in our mind's eye waiting until the moment arrives to go forward in such an enterprise. The writings of the books are a deliberate collaboration between all of us to serve not only you but untold nations, as well, in evolution. In turn, we have united with you because you agreed in the inner realms (higher levels of consciousness before incarnating and often visited during sleep time) as well as the outer realms (lower level of consciousness) to serve for the highest good.

"In the higher realms of Light, several teams of great standing have been formed to uplift you throughout your endeavors on Earth. Telbar is one such group, of which many of the Akasie family members have joined for purpose to see you through your ascension to the fifth dimension this go-around in your physical form. You know what I say is highly possible and I wish for you to take this information into your conscious awareness, anchoring it securely into your reality. This has been planned in the inner realms by all of us, the Akasie and by you. We desire dear one, sweet Nakala, that you come home to us at last.

"You came to Earth such a long time ago. I say you came for the experience to express through the physical form. But that wasn't the only reason. You came here long ago to assist those who had come and had begun to lose their sense of Oneness. In other words, they had embraced another way: the sense of separation, which by the way is nothing more than an illusionary concept created by the human ego.

"Nakala, I give it to you that you have a multitude of Light Beings at your beck and call to assist you on your path. But first, dear one, you must, ask, allow, and accept. To ask with sincerity (always with the intention that you receive what it is for your highest good); to allow the answer to come forth (it may come in a form that you do not expect and may not be easily recognized); and to accept, with gratitude, the assistance, Nakala, from those of the higher realms—your teachers—your guardians. We know, Nakala, what is best for you always.

"But Nakala there is another aspect to all of this. You are being retrained to listen to your heart. For such a long time, and I must include that through a multitude of embodiments on this Earth, you have suffered a steady decline in following the promptings received from your heart—its yearnings. There were times, dear one, when you weren't able to follow simply because you were held hostage in some way or another by another person or persons. This was not of your making but it still had a profound impact on you as your self-expression—God's Will—answering your heart's song had been stifled. Throughout the ages this has occurred. One last thing on this, Nakala: oft times when someone has been imprisoned in some manner, the experience can break the spirit, it is so profound or traumatic. Healing must take place before you will regain you footing on your spiritual path.

"One must always ask to receive a gift such as this. We came to you with words of the esoteric teachings of which you have never heard before. For you, the wanting of such knowledge has been immeasurable, the push to receive never ending. Even so, our sudden appearance caused quite a stir!

"I tell you, all must be in alignment to begin the communications to anyone on the Earth plane. Even then, we must tread lightly. We wish not to cause fear or panic with our presence. You are of a delicate nature, like a flower. When you first open, the flower wilts easily.

"I am one of those who assisted in the giving of the gift to you. You wonder what I mean when I talk of the gift. The gift is to open to receive the transmissions from those who are of a higher level of intelligence and from the higher realms of Light. On many occasions you have given yourself over—prostrate—receiving our radiation. We assisted in the activations of brain pathways by the way of neurons and receptors. In other words, we did a little rewiring in the cranial cavity so you would be able to hear us and channel our communications to others. We have the knowledge and the ability. This is how it is done.

"What a time it has been! There has been much upheaval in all areas of your life. During this time, we witnessed the making of much negative emotion by you because you did not have the full realization that we had come to teach. We saw fear being birthed because of the many modalities in which we chose to teach! Sometimes our teachings came across a bit unusual and maybe even a bit eccentric. Some teachings, we were told by you, much later, were unrecognizable as teachings even! We can laugh about this now, can't we, Missy? Many times, you said that you would never teach in the manner we had chosen. But I tell you we got our point across and that point came across quickly.

"Very early on in the communications I revealed to you that you were to document our communications, the experiences you had with us and with those on the Earth plane during your days. As your Master Teacher and Father, my authority prevailed with clarity, "We will be writing a book." It was then I gave you the name of our first book, *When Angels Speak.*"

"There was no question in the depths of your heart and soul as to the authenticity of my message and my direction. When I spoke of writing a book, for you it was a poignant awakening of a memory that had lain dormant for many years. What I disclosed revealed a key piece of information to your life's purpose—your heart's desire.

"We were in the infancy of an endeavor that would assist mankind, as well, as take you to ascension."

After Quem's dictation I heard him say, "You are to go into meditation tonight. Relax the mind."

CHAPTER
SEVEN

"Nakala, there is one more subject matter of importance that I would like to cover before we lay down the writings for the day," Quem began.

I remained quiet as I waited for Quem to shift his focus on the next subject he wanted to address.

"Together in Oneness, I stand beside many of my brothers and sisters as we bring forth this knowledge. There is a large group of Pleiadians who have come here to assist the people of this land, the Earth, to a higher awareness. I desire to explain—to make it known that I with Sarah, my wife, and our dignitaries, often travel to and from, going back and forth from the Earth to Pleiades and other Star Nations as well, in service to the One. I am one who leads many people in the Kingdom of Myra and because of my position, I must see to them as often as I can.

"As a people, we have evolved much. We are great leaders of this galaxy, members of the Galactic Federation and various councils for the purpose to lift the peoples up and assisting in evolution. We offer our knowledge, wisdom, and our love to teach you in areas that will take you further on your way as you travel into the Light joining your Christ Consciousness.

"We are from the stars, Nakala, just as you are.

"At this time I wish to explain that millions of years ago the Pleiades were a single planet. The planet was struck by a meteor; blasting it into bits and pieces, creating what is now called a system of stars which is now referred to by your astronomers as the Seven Sisters. There are many more stars that make up the Pleiades than the seven that the peoples of the Earth presume to make the entire system. Some of the Stars are inhabited; others, presently, are not.

"The meteor was driven into our land, our Star, for the purpose of destroying it—destroying us. However, our land was not completely destroyed, nor were we. Yes, severely injured, greatly injured. This occurred long ago and we have made peace with our adversaries; and our land has nearly healed in entirety, although there are scars of the impact that remain visible.

"At the time of the tragedy many of us had been evacuated in star ships. Yes, there were those who came to our aid.

"The purpose of my words here is to explain our mode of travel. For you, the following information is sure to ease somewhat as I have remained aloof with this data for several years. It is time, Nakala that I give unto you these words that are meant to be shared with all.

"You have received bits of information that alluded to Star Beings who have great knowledge and ability to travel by thought (through mind control). This information is correct. This can be done individually or in groups. There are also Star Beings who use several modes of transportation. One is teleportation and another is by use of Star Vehicles.

"The ships that you see in the skies today are purposely being revealed. Know there are cloaking devices and other ways to trick the mind into not seeing what is right before you. Full disclosure is at hand: you are to see—to realize that you are not the only ones here. We have been about for eons without the knowledge of the collective. However, be it known that there have always been those who have seen—always those who have known of our presence—those who serve the One alongside us who are walking in the bodies of flesh…like you.

"The purpose of this disclosure is to make it known that there are forces beyond your present outer knowing and to become comfortable with this knowledge.

CHAPTER
EIGHT

"You do not fully understand the importance of your name change."

"Wait Quem," I interjected, "This is a huge topic. I do not believe you have even mentioned this before."

"No, Nakala, I have not. This subject has not been open for review until this moment. Even though your name change took place in January of 2012, I have not spoken of the reasons, no, not in entirety.

"Nakala, when I was first allowed by law to communicate telepathically with you, your name had been Jackie Mullinax. After channeling our first book, *When Angels Speak* and going through the steps to get it edited and self-published/printed, I came to you and directed you to change your name.

"Personally, you felt that decision, my directive, was in error. You reasoned that all of the books written should be published under one name, your new name. You examined our directives, the timing of all therein. In your view, as limited as it is, we should have either waited to get *When Angels Speak* published to incorporate your new name or change your name before the book was written. You toyed with changing your name on the finished book, which would involve many steps. Ultimately, the choice was made to leave it as is because you were bound by contract with a self-publishing company. In other words, to change the name on that book would have taken a sizable sum of money to accomplish. The issue caused you an enormity of grief, as you felt, logically, my decision to publish under the name Jackie Mullinax was erroneous. Not so, my Nakala.

"*When Angels Speak* was given to and through you for a variety of reasons, to learn the ropes, if you will. Being a first time writer, as you found out, is a process encompassing several comprehensive steps to learn and complete, in order, to have a finished book ready for market. I wish not at this time to go into the steps as this is not the purpose to this chapter, or of this book.

"During all phases of completion of that book you were being trained and tested.

"As you acquire and integrate the teachings, there are always opportunities given to go further in your studies—to excel if you will—to make stronger your countenance. These opportunities are given and viewed as tests. Our questions—the tests you were given were, 'Would you continue to make yourself available to our teachings? Would you discipline yourself with your writing? Would you be strong enough in this area to stay with the project to completion? Would you continue to listen to our directives even though some may have seemed incongruent?' These were merely some of the areas we were working with you on.

"I assured you that I knew what I was doing by allowing, *When Angels Speak* to be published under the name of Jackie Mullinax. I assured you that book had been written by that person, Jackie Mullinax, the person you had been at the time. Honey, you have shifted in a radical manner. In addition, you had filed for divorce. We had full faith that you would continue to proceed with the writings; and the group Telbar had planned to gift you with your new name when, *When Angels Speak* was ready for distribution. By the way, Nakala Akasie is the name you are known by in the higher realms of Light. In addition, the probability of remarrying is in the mix. Always you are evolving, expanding higher into the Light.

"The name that I presented to you, Nakala Maria Angelic Akasie, was a gift to you, a tribute from the group Telbar to acknowledge the discipline you had developed, not only, but the acknowledgement that you had persevered with our teachings and had integrated them on a conscious level to the extent that you had developed new beliefs and new habits in your life. Your new name, Nakala, which I had asked you to take, was intended to remind you of your connection with the higher realms and your faithfulness to thy service to God.

"The name Nakala Maria Angelic Akasie, as I said before, is the name those of the higher realms know you by. The name Nakala is charged with a much higher vibration than Jackie.

"In addition, for you to follow my directives to legally change your name was a complicated matter; one that took courage and diligence to satisfy the courts. For you this was a great accomplishment. The Telbar, as with those in the heavenly realms, applaud your effort, Nakala.

"I say now that you are my daughter for those readers who have not picked up any other volume that we have contributed as of late to society. My wife, my Divine complement, Sarah and I, long ago, decided to give parenthood a try. Our way differs somewhat than what you experience on Earth. We will explain in another volume intended to be written and shared exactly what "parenthood" entails to the Pleiadian citizen.

"Nakala, many times over, I have given to you this phrase or expression: 'Nakala, you are my daughter only.' This is a term of endearment—my way of giving forth my love. You have heard it many times. The phrase has somewhat perplexed you as you have been told that I have children many. When you first began receiving our transmissions you were given a partial genealogy of the Akasie family. With this data, the genealogy, you saw that you were and still are a part of our family and an integral part for that matter! You are of Pleiadian origin.

"Some of the family members have remained in the Pleiades—some specifically in the halls of the Kingdom of Myra; others have come to earth either to incarnate in the human form or to assist those who have incarnated in human form. (We work together during the evolutionary shifts taking you to the fifth dimensional level of consciousness.) Others have traveled to other star nations, systems, even other galaxies to learn and to experience anew! We are travelers, Nakala.

"Go now to your book shelf containing the many journals that house the messages of the masters, archangels and Akasie family members. I say retrieve the book I spoke of with the genealogy therein, Nakala. I have a gift for you."

I sat for a moment before I rose from my office chair to get the book my father had sent me after. I couldn't imagine what *gift* I might receive. It is my father, Quem's character to gift me as he teaches me. His gifts are little tidbits of information, but nevertheless quite valuable. Sooner or later he will disclose the last fragment of the mystery that will reveal to me the entire picture, message, or teaching.

With me Quem has used this method often enough, the results being so profound that for some reason, at this time, I wanted to sit with it. On an intellectual level, I understood that I was about to receive a vital piece of information. On an emotional level, though, I wanted the full measure of his love. It was like savoring the arrival of something incredibly special that I had waited for such a long time. No longer a child, I did not grow impatient. I wanted the moment to last. *What gift could he possibly be referring to? Which journal would contain the information I required?* Silently, I asked Nathanal to please guide me to the correct book.

As I scanned the spines of the journals I was directed to look at the very bottom of the stack. It was labeled with the earliest date. Over the years, the stack had grown high and heavy, and it took some doing to retrieve it without causing the entire pile to tumble over. As I held the book in my hands, memories emerged of the early days when I had just started to hear the guides speak to me—when I had been so eager to learn…so eager that I literally could not rest from it all. Hence I had suffered from sleep deprivation and even questioned my sanity.

Slowly, I flipped the pages to the back; and as I did, I saw the pages of names that I had recorded: all of the beings who had come by and telepathically introduced themselves to me. Tears sprang to my eyes as I reread them. Over and over, I had contemplated the meaning of all the communications, never coming to a solid conclusion.

Then I found the page I was looking for…the page with the Akasie genealogy. The genealogy spanned four generations. I quickly scanned the page, concentrating on the record of names under Quem and Sarah's and saw what I had been looking for…the names directly listed under them: the names of their children. The first name that had been recorded was Cathryn Sebise Akasie, mine, which Quem had given to me long ago. I counted nine names after mine that all began with the letter T. Most all of them sounded like masculine names, but not all. *What had Quem meant when he had used the phrase that I was his daughter only? The statement puzzled me. Did he use that way of speaking to all of his children? Surely he had more than one daughter.*

For several minutes I stood there immersed in my thoughts staring at the names. One of the names listed had been Tirclé, a female guide who had worked with me for a few years. Tirclé had channeled artwork, but mostly, for me, she had channeled portraits. She had chosen the media of pencil to draw the likeness of some of the guides, archangels, and masters that I had been working with at the time. I had even received a few portraits of beings that were from Star Sirius. Others had been identified as being members of the Galactic Federation or a council that had not been identified to me.

I did not realize that I had gone away—been daydreaming—lost in thought when I heard Quem's voice, his words. "I have given you several moments to think over what you have been given." He paused for a moment then continued, "I saw and felt the gratitude expand as you thought of those beings—those memories—those beautiful portraits of those who have dedicated their lives in service to Our God, Our Creator, Our Light!

"My gift, Nakala, I give to you now." Instantly, I felt myself sit up straight to receive as someone else took command of my body. The top of my head, my crown, began to tingle and I felt my vibration quicken. Then I felt the pressure of someone massaging my neck. I felt the stiffness as he maneuvered my neck and heard it crack several times. In my inner sight I saw a presence of a man wearing a white linen robe. He stood behind me massaging my shoulders and using his thumbs to press on certain spots. I hadn't noticed how sore I had become. I wondered if this might be Quem's gift. Then instantly I knew it wasn't. The gift was still to come. Then I felt a single deep breath being channeled through me and I relaxed, allowing the book to drop into my lap landing with a soft thud.

"Nakala," I heard, "listen to my voice, my words, please. What I have for you is a bit unusual—a bit unorthodox. Your brother, David, who passed from his earthly body several years ago, is of the Akasie family."

His words, sharp and unsettling couldn't have surprised me more. I wanted to shut out Quem's words, his message. So many years had passed. I wanted to forget. I wanted to pretend it hadn't happened. But I could not.

The anger surged and I shuddered. My body began to feel hot and I felt my face, neck, and chest flush. I wanted to erase what Quem had said... all the unpleasant memories, the disappointment. I wanted to be finished with all of that. Apparently I wasn't.

"Nakala, I am asking you to allow yourself to be with this information. Your brother is of our family. He is your Pleiadian brother, Nakala. Perhaps you may in time learn to accept this as truth." "Father, you mean he is your son? Is this what you are saying?"

Instead of speaking to me, Quem chose to communicate by projecting an image. With my inner sight, I saw Quem nod his head, yes. Next, I saw Quem make a movement with his hand much like sign language or playing the game Charades that meant, "I speak the truth."

Patiently, I waited for Quem to say something else related to subject but he had settled into a stillness that I felt inappropriate to impose upon.

Immediately, I worked to process Quem's disclosure. My heart had been closed regarding the matter. I knew for my health and peace of mind that I must work through my thoughts and feelings and that it might take me a good while to accept in its entirety.

Swiftly, the silence was broken. Quem's voice held steady as he spoke, "Nakala pick up the journal, please." I did as he told me, opening it near the back of the book, thinking he wanted me to look at the genealogy again. I wasn't able to readily find that page as I had before. As I looked through the pages for the genealogy, I noticed the names that I had written down and how many pages of them there were! Without any thought to why Quem had directed me to get the book, I decided to take a closer look at the names of those who had come to introduce themselves to me during those first few months. Then more out of curiosity I decided to get an estimate of how many beings had come, so I did some quick math, coming up with 238 entries. I counted each line as a single entry even though some lines had several names on them. On each line I had written the date of their visit (covering a five month period) and what title they held. Some were masters, some had said they were overseers, some archangels, some had identified themselves as being an 'angel most high'. I saw that some of the names had been recorded more than once as they had visited on several days.

Every time I looked at those pages I felt such an overwhelming sense of love and gratitude that my heart expanded, and the tears welled up and spilled over. The book itself represented constant support and devotion from the Beings of Light. The love I had received and continue to receive supersedes all expectation.

As I continued to turn the pages I noticed something a little different. There were two pages that I had written—affirmations to be precise—outlining the perfect husband I had wanted to bring in to my life. I heard myself sigh as I reread the attributes, skills, over-all appearance, and habits that I desired in my dream mate. Then I asked, "My Father, what is it you want me to see…to receive? The gift you speak of? What more could I possibly receive?"

"Nakala," Quem began, "You see the pages you wrote long ago when you wanted to bring in a husband, one that was befitting a queen? Won't you read them again?" I did as he asked and once again I felt a deep desire rise up within me to have a companion. My divorce wasn't final; yet I had been without a mate whom I resonated with on my spiritual journey for my entire thirty-five year marriage. If there were even a miniscule chance that I would be gifted with a mate, I had wanted to be certain that I drew in the perfect man as God intended.

"Nakala, *He comes,*" was all Quem said. I knew what he said was true, yet I wanted to know *when.* I wanted Quem to provide me details. *What was his name, his age, where would I meet him, and most of all what did he look like?*

Quem politely but firmly stated, "Nakala, soon you will have the *One* to fulfill.

Slowly I got up from my desk and stretched. It had been a long afternoon of writing with Quem. I told Quem that I really could use some time to myself as I thought I should process some of what I had been given to write. Besides, it was near dinnertime. I wanted to rest for a few minutes before I went into the kitchen to prepare dinner. I had gone into the living room and had just sat down when I heard my name, spoken like it was being posed as a question, "Nakala?" Because only my name had been said, I wasn't able to pick up anything unique like his tone or accent (all beings have their subtle ways of communicating) to recognize the speaker; so I asked, "Who is this?"

"Nathanal. It is me. It is time that I address our relationship. I am guide to you. You have known me *always*. I tend to you. All personal requirements I see to. All travel preparations I see to. I guide you in your daily steps. Know this…I am your twin flame: your divine complement."

Even though I had heard Nathanal speak of being my twin flame before, I paused to review my feelings concerning the matter. I took note that ever since I had begun to hear the Beings of Light speak to me, Nathanal had always been with me. I had always felt comfortable with him and had grown to appreciate and depend on him on every level. And, I did love him but it wasn't a starry-eyed, all-consuming love that I felt for him like I'd thought I *should* feel toward a twin flame. I had known of Nathanal for several years now and this feeling had not developed. *Why not?*

Suddenly, I was taken back to Quem. I felt his desire to give forth something of great importance.

"My gift to you, Nakala, is this: know that there are many steps coming your way, many upheavals on the horizon. I state it this way because this is the way that you believe significant changes to be in your life. Because you are of the appearance world, you will view it in this manner. Just now, I caution you! These steps that come are necessary to bring you closer to coming home—reclaiming the knowledge and mastery that is your Divine heritage! I am your father and I watch over you in all you do. As Master, I know your path intimately and I assure you that *soon* you will have on your arm the *One* who will sweep you off of your feet. He is your perfect complement on the sphere of Earth. Know that as complement he will exchange ideas and energy on numerous levels of consciousness for the rest of your days as an unascended being. You know him and have worked and continue to work with him on inner levels and throughout many of your sojourns on Earth (embodiments)."

A wave of frustration hit and I heard myself speak in a tone I did not recognize as my own, "*Soon?* What do you mean *soon?* I have heard this word, *soon*, used on many occasions by you and the others who guide me. I feel its meaning is ambiguous." Quem channeled another breath through me before answering, "When all is in alignment. This is when you will be mated."

An involuntary sigh escaped my lips. My feelings were of a mixed sort, almost as if I had been split into two people. I recognized in my body the heavy feelings of disappointment settling in for having been given such a vague message. I knew that my ego had taken control and had chosen to focus on the vague aspect of the message. Quem had given me a shred of hope…not much, I surmised, but still…Purposefully shifting my thoughts, I purposely reexamined Quem's message choosing to view it in a positive manner—the one of hope and promise of what is on the horizon—and I gave thanks for the love of it all…what the Akasie were doing for me. I knew when the time was correct I would find true love.

CHAPTER
NINE

The day had begun with an early meditation followed by my prayers and affirmations before I moved into the kitchen for a bite to eat. Samuel Paul, one of the Akasie Ascended Masters telepathically stated while I was preparing my meal that he wanted to "give me words". As a joke, I answered that I would head back into the office, soon. We both laughed. Then he reminded me that the day before I had set the intention to modify some of my affirmations.

Rewriting my affirmations was something I certainly wanted to accomplish, but I felt it more crucial that I have a conversation with one of the masters concerning my feelings toward Nathanal. The dialogue yesterday had brought up some questions. Namely, why hadn't I ever felt an intense attraction or connection to Nathanal? Was it because I couldn't physically see him? Energetically, I feel him…his love.

Out of the blue, I heard Nathanal say, his voice deep with emotion, "Nakala, I love you more than life itself." Then I heard a thump on my wall. (This is one of the ways my guides make an emphasis on a statement.)

My heart expanded from hearing his romantic sentiment; but I still asked, "Nathanal, how could you love me more than life itself? I mean really is that possible?"

"Oh, yes!" Nathanal responded in a husky tone indicating his deep and unwavering devotion and respect for me. Then he unexpectedly pledged, "Nakala I would give my life for you if that were possible in this very moment. I am not of the physical as you are. Yet, I know, I see, I feel all that you are about. I explain. You are my counterpart and because you reside in the physical realm you feel the dense energies to a point that it overrides your ability to see or experience so much of the beauty that is before you! I alongside many others are constantly giving forth to you radiation to assist you throughout your journey in the flesh.

"You are open to receiving the directives, not only from us but from your heart! You recognize the communications—the commands that the God in you is giving—the choices that are set before you in order to follow your Divine path during this lifetime. You remember who you are Nakala…yet you continue to allow the ego to make many choices instead of following God's Will.

"We continue to work with you as your spiritual structure becomes stronger. Overall you are more knowledgeable, wiser, and able to hold more Light throughout your journey, not only at this time of embodiment, but always. Nakala, you are part of an otherworldly network, the family of Akasie, from the star system of Pleiades. We are Beings of Great Light who have come to this Earth to promote healing for all thereon. We have pledged our lives to this cause. Healing, Nakala, encompasses vast and it is this term 'healing' I use to be interchangeable to remembering your true essence—your God-Self. This remembrance will take you to the fifth dimension—to your ascension. I say, Nakala, you are nearing the moment when you receive the banner of Lady Master, taking your ascension, which is a mite different than merely the occasional rise to the vibration of the fifth sphere. As you acquire mastery you have the choice of joining the Great White Brotherhood in service to those who reside on the Earth Sphere. This is a unique opportunity, one not lightly spoken of.

"Nakala I know your heart—your chosen path. I know my chosen path which is the same as yours." At that point, Nathanal stopped speaking and I felt a wave of emotion that was akin to sadness, yet I knew it wasn't mine.

"Nathanal? What is it? Is what I feel *your* sadness? Are *you* sad?" In my mind's eye, I saw Nathanal picking at his fingernails as if he were nervous or avoiding me. Then I saw him steal a glance in my direction. He saw that I was watching him.

Slowly, Nathanal lowered his hands to his sides. It seemed to me I could see the impression of Nathanal…perhaps a knowing of some sort…his curly dark brown shoulder-length hair. Nathanal wore an off-white colored linen tunic with a high collar and pants of the same shade of fabric with brown sandals. I could tell he didn't have facial hair but was unable to see any of his features in detail. His skin was white like mine. He was a taller man, more on the lean side.

The image of the portrait that Tirclé had channeled through me of Nathanal came to my mind. When he had posed for Tirclé, he had worn his hair much shorter and had chosen to present himself without a shirt. He had looked to be in his twenties in that portrait…his appearance was of youth. He had worn the Akasie necklace in the middle of his chest—the huge emerald. It hung from a bold gold chain.

In the drawing, I had been limited, not receiving the full effect. Even though I could only use my imagination as to the true appearance of the Akasie Emerald, the stone had looked exceptional and one of great worth.

Just then Nathanal projected the image of the necklace into my mind; and I saw the gold chain the gemstone hung from. It was crafted with alternating gold discs connected by little jump rings, also gold. The discs were approximately ½ inch in diameter. Each disc had some sort of ancient symbol etched on it.

The emerald, brilliant in color and clarity, had a faceted hexagonal cut, set in a gold filigree bezel. The piece looked ancient, but retained a magnificence that appeared timeless. The size of the stone was impressive; and as near as I could tell, it was well over one inch in diameter and lay precisely over the middle of his chest. I had seen Quem wear an emerald necklace of similar style, or possibly identical, the last time I had seen him.

Often, I had wondered if the portraits I had received were accurate or merely a close likeness. Did Tirclé have her subjects pose or had she channeled them by memory? I am not sure she had ever said.

Recently, Quem had told me that Tirclé had decided to re-embody and was not available to work with me any longer.

Something nudged me back from my reverie. Putting my attention back to Nathanal, I saw that he had remained fixed, his attention on me, exactly where he had been standing, motionless. He had good-naturedly waited for me to come back to him. Again, I asked him, "Was the sadness I felt earlier yours?"

As he nodded his head, yes, I sensed that perhaps he didn't trust himself to speak, not just yet anyway. Not knowing what to do, I sat still and waited for Nathanal to address my question. In my mind's eye, I saw Nathanal move toward the couch and I thought for a moment he may sit down next to me, but instead he chose to sit down on the far end of the couch. He turned his body toward me indicating that he wanted something. Perhaps he just wanted to look at me.

"Nakala," Nathanal began. Then I heard him make a sound like he was clearing his throat. "I'd like to state that yes, you are quite able to pick up our emotions. You feel my love, do you not? Then why wouldn't you feel my sadness?"

"Well," after I had paused long enough to think his statement through, I said, "Nathanal, I wasn't sure you ever felt sad!"

"Oh, yes, there are times aplenty that I feel…sadness that is. I look at you, your beauty, and so want to take you in my arms and just hold you. There are times that I see you crying…"

I saw him shake his head as if he wanted to erase those memories that seemed to haunt him so. Then he bowed his head into his hands and remained there for a few moments. Abruptly, he sat up straight then looked deeply into my eyes and declared, "Nakala! I love you! To see you suffer… this brings tears to my eyes. My heart aches at times as I watch you go through particular trials!"

Not sure how to respond, I remained motionless. We both sat with our own private thoughts for several minutes longer. I was totally out of my comfort zone by hearing that Nathanal felt like this. Then I saw him rise and scoot closer to me.

I wasn't sure how to proceed with what Nathanal had revealed. Even so, it was I who finally spoke, breaking the silence. Taking a chance, I dove in and said, "So…you feel my emotions…you witness all that I think, feel, and do!"

"Yes, Nakala, there are no secrets…although I can and do at times choose to set my attention elsewhere! But I feel…all."

CHAPTER
TEN

Early the following morning Quem asked me to sit and take his words—his teaching. Yesterday had been a full day of writing with Quem and I couldn't imagine what Quem would have to add to his previous teachings. He began by saying, "I'd like to continue on with my words—the beginnings of your awakening to the gift of becoming a full channel and servant of God. Our work together has just begun.

"Shortly after you began to work with the pendulum you began to hear our words—our messages. It was a transitory experience: a step forward if you will. Always you are gaining new insights and skills as you access higher levels of illumination, knowledge, and wisdom.

"You could hear us speak to you; but as a novice the communications seemed surreal—to the point of being fantastic and unbelievable. Since you were having difficulty believing yourself in what was happening to you and through you, how were you to share your experiences with others—your closest friends and family members? For some time you were unable to share your experiences with anyone. In essence, you hid this knowledge from everyone. Fear ruled your thoughts and feelings concerning this revelation. We heard as you examined your plight in every conceivable angle of the situations at hand. Your desire was to present your new ability to your friends and family. Always, it came to this: How would they accept your story?"

"We understood your reluctance. However, we had to move you forward as fear will not lift you into the Light; fear takes you deep into the darkness."

"You were chosen channel; and in order to get you up and running, we had to direct you to face your fears, some of which had embraced you tightly in life to the point of breaking you, Nakala. Your fears affected your decisions.

"For a good while you continued to use the pendulum to communicate with us. We had expected this and felt it to be fine as with any transition there is usually an overlap of energies. In other words, as a general rule, a person will continue to use one level of a skill as he or she is learning and integrating a higher level of that same skill. It is like learning to play the piano. Often beginners will be given flash cards to learn the notes. Later those cards are superfluous as the student has integrated that knowledge, allowing himself or herself to advance further, becoming more skilled at his endeavor.

"Like the teacher who will at one point take away the flash cards from the piano student, we gave you the directive to lay down the device—pendulum—as it was not desirable for you to use when we moved you to the next level of your gift. We began to encourage you to trust yourself as you practiced your proficiency in channeling our messages with the voice. The device—the pendulum—for you, was limiting, keeping you captive and unsure of yourself. We had to wean you off of this tool, Nakala. It was to be as this was for the highest good.

"The pendulum is without a doubt a tool that may be of assistance in many areas. But for you it had been merely a stepping-stone to get to the place of clairaudience: the ability to hear and channel the beings who reside in the higher realms of Light.

"I desire to add that the pendulum is used as a device to go forward (to learn the control of energy) not only for you but by the students of Light (upcoming spiritual guides). You see Nakala, *all* are learning. The pendulum serves as a way for them to learn to concentrate and focus—to ready them to work as a guide for someone such as you. You had questioned earlier, during the workshop, why some of the people were having difficulty connecting to the energy of the pendulum. This is why.

"As part of your daily protocol, when you are working at communicating with the Masters and Beings of Light, we, the Akasie, highly recommend you say your prayers and affirmations first thing upon awakening from your night's sleep. Always affirm that you are working with the Highest Most Divine Creative Awareness (your Mighty I AM Presence), or you may end up having a similar experience or perhaps one that may be a bit more of a challenge. It is always best that you have Divine guidance in your spiritual communications. When you do not set a particular intention, you are in essence inviting communications from anyone who happens by.

"There are many different energies or spirits who may be of a lower vibration that may come forth when you are using a spiritual tool, such as a pendulum.

"In addition, many of the beings who came by and introduced themselves were not masters themselves and had not come to teach you for your highest good. Many came by to greet you, as when one such as you opens to the communications, this is cause for much celebration in the higher realms of Light. There were those who had the desire only to converse. Others still came and possibly presented themselves as a nuisance or even as a sort who held the intent to create upheaval.

"The pendulum is a tool used to bring forth unseen forces—energy much like your Ouija board. We tell you to always use extreme caution when calling in any entities. This is for your protection, as well, as the protection for those who are about you. This information is particularly important to know and to follow! People sometimes jump into places they are not prepared for or don't belong in; the actions of not using careful consideration may result in an unhealthy or even a dangerous situation.

"In this work, our aim is to make it perfectly clear that this experience, your experience, had been allowed! One of our tasks as masters is to teach and guide; another is to protect those in our charge. We make it known when you get off track or you are not listening to your heart. We may use extreme measures or employ unusual tactics to allow you the opportunity to see that you are doing something that is not in balance with Spirit. All spiritual beings in physical form have free will. Because of this you may look at any given situation and decide what it is you want to do: what is your best choice? In any given circumstance, you must listen to your heart to find the solution that is correct for you, bringing balance and harmony to your life. The correct answer is always within your grasp.

"Because masters, archangels, and experienced spirit guides have the ability to communicate with all levels of your being, specifically your higher consciousness, we knew it was your time. We were to assist in this grand event, taking the situation in hand for what it was, working with it for the highest good of all concerned. Yes, we most certainly did assess all possible outcomes to what was occurring. We love you. Know this for it is truth.

"We had created a detailed curriculum with practical, precise and individualized teachings. Our main concern at this time had been to teach you, Nakala, not only to affirm that you were working with the Highest and Most Divine Creative Awareness, but to teach you that you must totally believe that who works with you at all times loves you unconditionally, having the highest regard and respect for your welfare not only spiritually, but physically, emotionally, mentally, psychically, in all dimensions, in the cosmos, always and everywhere.

"In order to direct you to completion in your understanding, you had to integrate a solid foundation in your heart connection that you work *only* with the Light Beings of the Most High. Through the unfoldment of your newly acquired gifts, you were allowed and assisted to communicate with earth-bound spirits, including your departed son. This was done for the purpose to assist in layers of healing. We also played the devil's advocate by allowing you to think you had been communicating with beings of much lower vibration. We played the part quite well by thumping on the walls and walking on the roof. Oh yes, we did other things as well. In essence, you fully believed that evil beings had taken up residence in your home. All of this was done in order to teach you the importance of following protocol!

"In this case the negative thought forms did not communicate, they controlled. Even though you continued to ask endless questions and receive contradictory answers, you were headstrong and persevered. Nakala, I say this stubborn streak is to be used to motivate you into action not prevent the union of the Christ consciousness.

"Repeatedly, when you had asked specific questions the pendulum indicated (unseen forces) that you were in the company of negative entities. Daily you worked with the pendulum to remove the negative entities only to have more seemingly appear, and at times they had grown in strength! Once fear comes into the picture, it has the tendency to grow into unmanageable proportions, becoming extremely powerful. What you had been doing was futile. It was time to make the transition from the pendulum to being full channel. We promoted the transition quickly!

"We will stop here and explain to the reader that when you are communicating with spirit guides, the only way to receive accurate answers is to clearly state your intention and ask your questions in a very specific manner. We repeat what Nakala has previously stated. If you do not ask questions properly, you will get answers that are inconsistent. We take your question literally word for word and answer each question in accordance to how the question is asked. The Akasie do not promise an absolute outcome to our answers to future questions ever! We will tell you the possibility and the probability of something that may occur, but that is as far as we go. The future is constantly in motion—ever changing, so we ask you please don't ask who your future wife or husband will be in ten years or perhaps how many children you will have. We cannot answer those questions accurately.

"This is an example of what may occur when a question is asked that is not specific enough. 'Will I receive a phone call from Tom today?' First off this is a future question. We would take that question and may answer you with a 'yes' because Tom is thinking of calling you. His thought of calling you creates a high probability that you will receive that call. Or we may choose to answer you with a 'no' because either Tom hasn't thought of calling you or is thinking of calling but hasn't decided. Even if he has decided, he may very well change his mind, get distracted, postpone the call until tomorrow, or simply forget all together. One must understand that you can ask the same question two separate times, and phrase the question exactly the same, but get two completely different answers. This is why Nakala got inconsistent answers on many occasions!

"As Nakala went deeper into her new found gift, she withdrew from many of her friends and family. Her social activities took a downward spiral, leaving every available moment she had to work with the pendulum.

"At the Dowsing Seminar, the teachings included how to work with all sorts of negative energy by releasing, transmuting it, and then filling the void created with love and gratitude. We are only speaking on the negative energies here, more clearly defined as negative entities, including how to check with the pendulum to see if there are any negative entities about and how to release them.

"Let's explain what a negative thought form or negative entity is. A negative thought form or a negative entity is an *energy* that has been created from negative thoughts—negative thoughts at the core are always derived by fear. They include but are not limited to anger, resentment, hate, and insecurity. When the energy frequency becomes strong enough, it is classified as an entity and has the capability of being seen in the aura of the creator or recipient of the energy.

"There are oft times when an opportunity presents itself and the entity will be magnetized to another person. Whoever the negative entity is attracted to (like energy magnetizes like energy) may be either the person who is creating negative thoughts and emotions or someone who is very vulnerable in specific areas. I repeat, like energies attract like energies.

"People who have negative thought forms or entities attached may exhibit any type of behaviors in any number of areas. I speak of being unbalanced in the physical, mental, emotional, and yes, the spiritual capacities. When you are in someone's company who is creating this type of energy, you may feel uncomfortable or distrustful or even a repulsion to them. If you are sensitive enough, you may pick up the actual emotions that are being exhibited: sadness, anger, abandonment, cynicism, desperation and so on.

"Again, I must state this in a strong fashion: Thoughts and emotions are very powerful. So powerful, in fact, are these energies that we have chosen this subject to place much of our attention on in this book.

"When a person has a negative thought form or entity attached, he will most assuredly suffer from feelings of anxiety and vulnerability. When you create negative thoughts, you of course are going to feel the negative emotions.

"We will go back to Nakala's case here. When she was working with the pendulum, she asked many questions that were not phrased accurately or specifically. Her basic assumptions or deductions had been that she was getting some sort of evil beings that were 'playing' with her. Because of her hypothesis, she had felt frightened. Nakala's thoughts had been negative or fear based. This is the beginning of creating a negative thought form or entity.

"As the days passed, the emotion of fear grew. These entities can and often do become extremely controlling. In fact, with many cases, these energies become so aggressive they may take possession or control of the person causing many undesirable behaviors. For instance, they may cause severe mood swings that typically encompass depression, anxiety, and anger. Negative entities may cause illness and in extreme cases, the energies can cause such instability that the person will surrender to self-mutilation or perhaps go insane. In some occurrences, we see homicide and/or suicide. There are many variations that have been experienced and observed with negative entity possession. Often you will see addictions, rage, abuse, bipolar symptoms, paranoia, depression, and suicidal tendencies.

"You see, when you have invested much energy thinking negative thoughts followed by negative feelings such as fear, insecurity, anger, unworthiness and so on, you lose control of your thoughts. As time goes on, if left unchecked, those thoughts and emotions become very strong and they take over like a whirlpool sucking you further down into the murky waters. In essence, you have given yourself over to be controlled by the negativity: to become more negative than positive. Your thoughts literally take control of you!

"Perhaps, you look at it like a pregnancy. You have conceived an embryo, which is a negative thought form or energy. In the prenatal period the energy is tiny and must be fed in order for it to survive and grow. Feeding it is giving it more negativity. In other words, you are focused on the negative of any given situation or what is wrong not the positive or what good may come out of the situation.

"In the early stages of learning self-discipline, it is easy to slip and not be vigilant of your thoughts. Take this as an example: this morning you overslept. You are supposed to be at work at 8:00 a.m. sharp. You rush to the bathroom to get ready and see that you have a pimple on your face and your hair doesn't do what you want. Your anxiety mounts. You just *know* there is no way you are going to get to work on time. As a rule, your boss will notice if anyone is not in their appointed station and busy. You worry that he will want to have "that talk" to flex his power. Traffic is horrendous and you end up parking out in "the sticks". As you head to your desk, you inadvertently run into someone who is talking about their teenager having an attitude; and you are reminded this very person gets on your very last nerve! You don't have the time or the patience for this interface! This is negative thought that is of course followed by emotion, my friends. You are feeding your embryo by nurturing it with anger, anxiety, and so on.

"As the embryo grows, it requires more negative energy or food. With more negative thoughts and emotions, the embryo grows into a fetus until it is time for it to be born. I am sure you know someone who seems very negative, so much so, that you may prefer to avoid their company. The person has either given birth to a negative entity or attracted one. The thoughts and emotions have grown so powerful with negative energy that the majority of what they are creating is negative! When this happens, you have tipped the balance and you are not in control of your thoughts or emotions any longer—they control you!

"We have discussed what negative entities are capable of. In Nakala's case, there was much fear of the negative entities themselves! Much attention was given to checking to see if they were about and releasing them. But we say here that with this behavior alone, Nakala was creating them herself. Unfortunately, she was blinded, left unaware of what she was doing. As the days passed, the fear grew and so did the negative energy. We tell you here, all is for purpose.

"Because this one has gone through this remarkable period in her life, we can share it with you in hopes that you will realize how incredibly powerful the energy of thought and emotion is."

✳ ✳ ✳

A few months into my lessons of using the pendulum to ask and receive answers, I began to put two and two together. I knew that it was better for me to stop depending on the device that was used for a basic level of communication. Even so I continued to use the pendulum like a crutch. Even though I had acquired the ability to communicate telepathically with the Beings of Light and I had been advised not to use the device any longer, I had continued to take it with me wherever I went and used it often.

Learning to become a channel had been challenging, and at times I felt like I was on overload. In other words, my head ached from the communications that were occurring at all times of the day and night! Sleep was something that had become a treasured gift.

Knowing all about the nature of being obsessive, I had become a little concerned about my activities. However, I had reasoned that if I was able to maintain appearances by keeping the house clean and tidy, the lawn cut, and the gardens weeded, that would prove my ability to stay grounded and there would be nothing to worry about.

Even though Quem and the other guides and masters offered their assistance, sometimes my head spun with this incessant pain from trying to keep up with the conversation that had been secretly going on in my mind. I began to question if it had been wrong of me to connect to a higher intelligence. I had wanted to know the secrets of the universe. I had wanted to know the origin of the beings who worked with me and what they were like. Understanding that I easily fell into conversations with the guides in the middle of the night when I was supposed to be sleeping was not beneficial, I continually weighed the pros and cons of what I was doing. Even though I saw that my health was at risk, I had simply refused to lay the conversations down. But this horrible fear continued to creep up. The answers I received had sometimes been inconsistent. Why? At the time none of it made sense. *What had really happened?* I had really been frightened. Sometimes I had thought I should stop talking to them all together! But always I rationalized and came to the same conclusion. I wanted to hear what they had to say! Mentally and emotionally I had become exhausted and felt much like a ping pong ball that was being bounced around, hitting the walls, the ceiling, the floor and then landing in a pool of thick mud! I had been paralyzed!

After I had decided to tell Beth about what was happening, she advised me to stop using the pendulum altogether and "For heaven's sake," Beth had stated emphatically, "stop talking to them!"

But my choice had not been to listen to her advice but had been to continue to communicate with the beings. I had been hooked. They had been teaching me things and I was receiving a wonderful energy. For me, there was no mistake that what they gave me…it was Love. As I continued to work with the Pleiadians, something amazing began to happen. I began to see a different type of communication. What I saw was movements or drawings in my inner eye. I can see it happen with my eyes open or closed and can only describe it like I am looking at a blank board or a screen and seeing a person write on it. I literally see the symbols or words being written on an invisible screen. The thing was, there wasn't a person, a board or any writing device.

In addition, my guides had begun to exercise my neck, shoulders and back by turning my head in different directions. Every morning they had worked with me explaining that they were assisting me in releasing the tension from my body. It was optimal for the blood to flow to the brain and all parts of my body. It had been like having a private massage therapist come to my room. I had been getting all of this great stuff at the same time I had continued to use my pendulum and had been receiving contradictory information and then…as I sat in my chair listening to music to relax, these beings began to dance with me by moving my head and or different parts of my body in different positions and at the same time giving me this beautiful energy that I now call, "love energy". This love energy expanded my emotional body as it coincided with the rhythm of the music. The beings, whoever they were, had exquisite rhythm, perfect timing….

All at once Quem began to speak to me, clearly indicating that I include his words in this area of the manuscript. "I am going to help you out here a bit," he said. "All beings of the higher realms have the ability to give energy (some refer to this energy as radiation) to anyone, anywhere, and at any time. As you know, everything is made of energy and everything has its own specific vibration. When we wish to dance with you, we create or feel an emotion, a particular level of love which is in itself a frequency. Your emotional body picks up this frequency and is felt in your physical body as a vibration. Your body feels the frequency that is being sent out from us and responds to it, creating its own vibration. This all depends on our level of love at the time.

"You have noticed that there are moments as you listen to a melody that you naturally emotionally soar higher. During this time together, we feel many levels of emotion. As you receive the energy from us, you are also individually resonating with each aspect of the music: the melody, tempo, pitch, and even the lyrics that you hear and feel. This is an expression of emotion. Honey, what we are engaged in is an energetic dance.

"Since we are connected to you on an energetic level of consciousness, we know when you are listening to your beautiful music. We can hear your music; we also feel the vibration of the music and the vibration of you, Nakala. We really don't hear it like you do. We do not reside in the third dimension.

"We must explain this to you. Remember, my dear one, of a time when a melody or a tune was stuck in your head. You heard the music, did you not? Over and over the music played. The sound was internal. It was the mind that gave you the music.

"Wait," I said, "Quem why do you keep saying 'we'? Who is it you are referring to?"

"Ah, Nakala, I speak for the entire group of Telbar. It is the group who is connected with you. I speak for all.

"Now we go on?" Quem asked. I took a deep breath, wondering how many members there were in this group called Telbar and nodded my head, yes.

…"When we wish to share our love with you, we do this by sending the love energetically to you. This is all done with our thoughts and emotions, Nakala. You feel a vibration, do you not? What happens is your body receives this energy, this love. In turn, you respond energetically to this love vibration that we are giving you by creating your own emotion that creates a vibration. This energy that you receive feels good, like love to you. It is a communication, a dance of positive energies, so you respond. In turn, we feel your emotion as well—your love and gratitude. As you know, it is quite beautiful!

"Positive emotion will manifest in a vibration that feels calm, grateful or loving. Simply stated, positive emotions feel really good energetically. The stronger the feeling behind the thought the stronger the vibration! However, you are only attuned to pick up an intensity that only goes so high.

"What we have been teaching with the dance is multifaceted. We chose to give you our love, this gift of positive emotion. Also, we have beckoned you energetically to join with us in the creation of positive energy.

"During these same occasions, we taught you to realize that when you listen to beautiful music, you are personally resonating and responding energetically to this music, these vibrations. Through your thought and feeling you are creating a powerful radiance into the cosmos for the angels to gather and distribute according to Divine Law.

"Sound is given to you through one of your physical senses and is of the physical world—the world of the material. When the sound is harmonious, it is beautiful and it brings you much pleasure. Through this beauty, you respond emotionally with love and gratitude lifting you up higher. This is an energetic dance. This is also a form of self-expression.

"In conclusion, I tell you that during our dance we were in a very high state of love. What we were accomplishing, in essence, was an exchange of gifts with each other by sharing this energy, this love. When you bring together two or more individuals, the energies created are magnified above and beyond what the two or more individuals can create individually.

"Through the dance on the physical level you are contributing to your sphere of consciousness—the collective consciousness—with a higher vibration. Because you have joined with us, your love is amplified 100 fold and we are not only gifting humanity but all who reside in the cosmos."

At that moment Quem had me look up the Bible verse about two or more people coming together in His name for purposes of confirmation to his teaching. *For where two or three come together in my name, there am I with them.* Matthew 18:20 (NIV)

...As I was saying, the vibration that I felt in my body increased or decreased according to what these beings were expressing energetically.

In addition, during some of the sessions I began to notice the vibration would move around in my body much like I was an instrument. With each note that was played, a different part of my body would sing, hum, or vibrate. Then I noticed that certain chakras would vibrate according to the pitch of the tone. What was being shared (the vibration) with me was perfectly synchronized with the music and was a beautiful complement.

Strange things continued to take place. The head movements became more focused. I didn't think I was totally crazy because I had heard of this phenomenon before in the recording of "The Law of Attraction", by Esther and Jerry Hicks. Esther channels Abraham who is a group of spirit guides. They had begun to communicate through her with the movements of her nose and voice, which is exactly like what I was experiencing.

"Nakala, dear one, it is good to speak of your experience because, quite honestly, for one such as you to go through these steps has been a frightening experience. You had no one in the physical realm to confide to that would support you through your ordeal. If there had been someone that you could have talked to concerning your experience, who had "been there", you would have known that your experience was to be expected."

The memories of all the odd ways the Beings of Light had communicated with and through me caused me to pause for a few moments and wonder what on earth could or would happen next. It would have been so very helpful to have had a person to share this stuff with. But I had been afraid to open up; and when I did, I was sorry that I had.

"Quem, yes, to have someone to talk to about what was happening to me would have been so helpful. I had hinted to my then soon to be ex-husband that I was doing energy work and had asked him strategic questions regarding his beliefs concerning angels, spiritual guides, and the like. My objective had been to ease into a meaningful conversation regarding the metaphysical and maybe add in some of my own experiences and what I was really practicing. I wanted to test the waters, so to speak.

"The fact was I was terrified to speak of my experiences. It was when you, Quem, gave me the directive to record channeled message specifically for Scott and present it to him that things got really dicey. I guess, though, that Scott had already formulated his opinion that I was mentally ill by then?"

Quem answered quickly, "Nakala, we had planned that you give Scott the recording of that channeled message earlier than it was actually given. You kept putting it off because of how you felt concerning your experience. The channeled recording was prepared and handed off for many reasons.

"Confronting your worst fear took first priority. You were to let go of that fear and move on. This was a great tool to openly reveal what you were into. And to answer your question, yes, after Scott had listened to that recording he felt he had (so called) concrete evidence that you were ill. So be it!"

The details of the event vivid, still fresh, flashed before me. My feelings being extremely delicate concerning the matter made it difficult for me to respond. Somehow I managed to say, "Yes, I remember meeting him in the kitchen as he came in from work one evening. I had handed him the recorder and asked him to listen to it. He stood there on one side of the counter as I safely stood on the other side watching him. I purposely stood opposite of him with the counter safely separating us. I wanted a barrier of sorts…a sense of protection. I also wanted to watch his body language as he listened to the recording of me channeling you, Quem; you had been so persuasive, adamant in fact, telling me, over and over, to give the message to him. I was literally shaking as I waited for him to push the off button.

"When he had shut the recorder off, he simply stated he wanted to go into the bedroom to change into something more comfortable. Nothing was said in regards to that recording for months. The result of that confrontation was incomplete leaving me feeling utterly shut out—shut down from not being able to talk to Scott about anything. Yet we coexisted for several months after that until I finally rose up from my fear and stated that we were no longer communicating. I felt that I *couldn't communicate* with him any longer. His response was, 'As long as we are being honest with one another.…I think you should see a specialist and have your brain x-rayed.' Momentarily stunned, I paused just for a few moments before I asked him, 'Why?'

"Boldly, he dared to look straight into my eyes and with a firm voice stated, 'I think you may have a brain tumor.' It was as if he had kicked me in the gut, the blow had been *that* painful and that devastating.

"He had known something was up for nearly a year and had not hinted or given a single clue as to his suspicions."

I felt the heat rise in my face and shook my head in disbelief before I concluded, "All this time and he had not indicated a single insight, Quem!"

I asked, "Quem, were you there beside me listening to that conversation between Scott and myself? Did you hear me politely refuse his request to see a specialist and then swiftly move into indignation and retaliation by stating I wanted a divorce?"

Not waiting for Quem to answer I continued, "In a single instant I saw the entire picture. He had kept his thoughts about my suspected *brain tumor* to himself for an entire year. I realized with full force that if I had actually had a brain tumor or any medical issue for that matter, I could have died during his time of silence. My conclusion: if he had truly loved me he would have addressed the situation long before that moment."

In a hushed tone, Quem interrupted me, "Nakala, dearest, we were all there supporting you the best we could."

For me, the entire scene had been ugly and had changed my life so dramatically that I had felt like I would never be whole again.

For the entire year both of us had kept our thoughts and feelings to ourselves concerning our fear of what had been happening right before our very eyes. No one had been brave enough to address my state of mind.

Except for the one channeled message I had shared with Scott, I had remained silent concerning any of my communications with the Beings of Light which encompassed ascended masters, angels, spiritual guides and those in spirit who came by for one reason or another.

Unbeknownst to anyone except a small circle of friends and Beth, my home had turned into this hub of activity that only I knew about. I had wanted to talk to my husband about it all but had speculated he would never be able to believe me. I had been correct to remain silent. I picked up the conversation again thinking that if I went over what had happened once again, possibly I would understand. "Seriously, he had made the deduction that since I had been hearing voices…this indicated something worthy of more than a first or even a second glance. His initial summation had been there was something seriously wrong with me, but he had been too afraid to come to me to address it."

"Nakala," Quem interjected, "that was the old paradigm. You also were in an area where few were believers of this phenomenon. May I add that few had ever heard of this type of communication?

"I will not disregard your thoughts and feelings concerning your relationship or during any part of it with your husband, but first I wish to explain this. During your awakening (the receiving of spiritual gifts) we were working to teach you different *ways* to communicate, as well as the law of cause and effect: *what you place your attention on creates your reality.* In addition, you were having unseen visitors at all hours of the day and night who were merely coming to say hello to you. We all were in celebration of your new-found ability to hear us. At the time you didn't realize this, but for us this had been a long time in the making!"

After a long pause Quem began to speak again, "Nakala, because of all the interested parties who visited you in all hours of the day and night, you began to fail. Lack of sleep will cause a myriad of issues. You were in the midst of learning some very important lessons concerning communications with the unseen: how to set and maintain your boundaries and how to discern who you were communicating with and if it were for your highest good."

"Thank you, Quem. I know you have been speaking about the different beings who were coming to greet me in those first few months and who I could telepathically hear. In retrospect, I realize this was an awesome gift, but at the time I didn't understand who all of these people were!"

"What you speak is not the whole of it. There were many who came to observe you, Nakala, and our teachings. There were also many who came to simply give forth their radiation—their love—never uttering a single word."

The love of it all washed over me and I just couldn't help it: the tears began to roll down my cheeks and drip off my face making tiny plopping sounds as they landed. I had been supported in ways I never knew of, possibly that I still do not understand.

"It would have been so much easier had I understood," I stated. "At night, I was awakened by who I thought were angels talking with me for hours at a time. I couldn't sleep, Quem. The guides, angels or whoever kept talking to me. I am not one to do well without sleep. During the day, when these beings would ask me to please sit down to receive energy that would sustain me, I was so grateful. They assured me that I would be all right. I gladly allowed and accepted. However, I felt as if I were like a fine crystal goblet that was teetering on an edge of a wobbly table…I swear if one more thing had happened….Honestly, I was so close to tipping over the edge and shattering into a thousand fragments."

Quem validated my feelings by saying, "You were extremely fragile during that time, Nakala, and could have easily broken. There are many who awaken to certain spiritual gifts, misunderstanding what has occurred in entirety. Some, it is sad to say, end up in hospitals and/or on medication to rid themselves of the voices and visions that are often viewed as an imbalance of sorts. People must be able to function in today's society. Honey, make no mistake; there *are* those who are mentally imbalanced and require this sort of attention.

"In Scott's mind his initial concerns were valid as he knew very little about metaphysics, Beings of Light, or the abilities and expansion of the Mind. Where was God in any of this, Nakala? Naturally with his conclusion he labeled your symptoms as some sort of medical malady; his reaction was fear…fear of the unknown. Nakala, for months he had questioned how he could possibly address this issue with you, as it was highly sensitive. He was so fearful of the ramifications that he chose to ignore the issue: he was unable to face it! This is common amongst those who are not in alignment with God. However, we are most grateful that his choice was to confront the issue (not remain silent any longer) as what he did assisted our cause."

"Oh, Quem, I wouldn't say that he confronted *any* issue! He merely reacted to my declaration that I was finished!"

"Nevertheless, Nakala, he did use his voice to speak his truth, however skewed it was. It still was his view; and because of this, we must respect him and allow him to go on his way.

"To go on…We were also teaching you obedience. You remember the night you were abruptly awakened from a sound sleep? Your heart's rhythm had been intensified as if you had experienced a night terror. Only you hadn't. This had been a arranged for a teaching on many levels."

"Of course I remember! How could I forget that, Quem? My breathing was erratic and my heart had pounded so hard that I thought it might explode! There had been absolutely no cause for the way I woke up feeling. I had lain there for several minutes working to calm myself by breathing deeply and slowly. Mentally, I worked to pinpoint the cause of my feelings that were of pure terror and panic! I could not think of a single reasonable explanation that would serve me in getting to the root of the problem. There had been no nightmares or outer disturbances. Finally, I had asked, 'What is happening?' I heard a voice, who much later I learned had been Esse, a female guide from Pleiades, sternly command me, 'You must get up and go downstairs now.' Regardless of my objections, the being didn't let up. She or he, I could not distinguish, persisted with, 'You must learn to trust.'

"In my agitated state of mind, again I sifted through my thoughts and feelings as to what might have caused me to feel such an awesome measure of terror—to make sense of the situation. Even though I felt an excruciating level of fear, I found no logical reason to rise from my bed and go downstairs. I argued with the being, 'Why would I want to go downstairs in the middle of the night? Am I in danger?' Then the being had directed me, 'Go into your office. Sit on the floor. Feel the energies.'

"After being pressured for some time, I finally did get up, grabbed a robe, and went on the upstairs landing to check the main living area for anything out of the ordinary. Of course, there was none. That night there was no reason for me to turn on a lamp to light my way. The moonlight poured in through the windows, creating a supernatural glow. So as not to disturb my husband, who was sleeping downstairs, I quietly crept down the carpeted stairs into my office. In the middle of the room, I sat down on the floor, instantly feeling a definite hum—a vibration emanating from beneath me as if my house were alive!

"That night the feelings of fear had run deep. The being, who remained nameless throughout the entire ordeal, explained that there is an electrical current, specifically a grid if you will, that runs from the electrical lines to each home. (In my neighborhood the lines were underground.) If all is still, you can feel it! I knew this but had never put any thought to it. After feeling the vibration I grew concerned about my physical welfare: the effect of this electricity that my body was receiving all the time.

"Also, during the lesson, it was explained that in the future if I were to receive any uncomfortable feelings that I considered immoderate, I should peel back the layers to find its origin: what the cause may be. The being had gone on to further warn me that if I, in the future, ever received such a feeling that intense again, I should immediately leave the area!

"Quem, I remember at that time I was on overload from constant communications. I could see that my lack of sleep affected my life on every level. My emotions were raw and had begun to wildly swing from one extreme to the other. One minute I was feeling this great love energy that I had been so grateful for. Do not get me wrong here. I appreciated the assistance. But in the very next moment I grew suspicious, fearful, and full of anxiety with surges of anger bubbling up to the surface. Because I hadn't known how to process what was happening, I began to direct my fear and anger toward the guides—you.

"In addition to the symbols, the dancing, and the voices, I had been receiving instructions on how to visualize and move energy in my body. What happened next was the breaking point for me."

I stopped talking to Quem. The memories were too fresh too painful. Then I heard Quem softly encourage me, "Nakala, it is good to talk about this. Continue please."

✳ ✳ ✳

I took a few deep breaths, not knowing if I cared to even try to go on, before I found the strength to go forward on the subject. "Well, in the evenings, for lengthy periods of time, I would be directed to sit at my desk to practice visualization techniques with different geometric shapes (energy) and move it. Through intention, I was able to see, feel, and direct the energy having color, shape, and density. As I continued to visualize, the energies would change, expand, and become stronger. This energy, beginning at the perineum (root chakra), would spiral up and around the spinal column (each chakra) going up through the crown chakra just above the top of my head. Then the energy would spiral back down around the spinal column once again in the opposite direction down to the root chakra. This action was repeated over and over, becoming stronger and faster. The intensity of this energy became so strong that it overpowered me. I remember asking what the purpose was. I don't remember who answered me; but they said, 'The purpose is to learn to have great focus.'"

Suddenly, I felt a deep breath being channeled through me as Quem stated, "I remember the question, Nakala."

"Quem, I had always felt that the answer, your answer was incomplete. Is this correct?"

In my inner awareness, I saw Quem nod his head, yes. Then another breath was channeled through me, then another.

"Nakala, dear heart, I tell you what you are ready to hear. I do not go into great elaborations of detail. When you are ready for more then you shall receive."

"Okay, I get it. I am on a need to know basis." Nice, I thought.

Quem answered me as if he had not heard the hint of sarcasm in my voice, "Yes, Nakala, our intention is to not overwhelm you with superfluous data. But to allow you to experience the shifts with our assistance—if you desire it that is."

"Oh, my, God! Are you serious? If I desire it? You know full well I desire your guidance, your assistance."

"Honey, at the time you did not have structure in your spiritual practice. We were teaching you the basics—the protocols.

Quem seemed to want to get to what I consider to be probably the most embarrassing event in my life and prompted me, "Go on Nakala, with your narrative."

As I hesitated a moment, it appeared that I was working to pick up where I had left off; but in reality I was working to gather my courage. "Okay. As I said before, as I was going through the experience, the power of the energy was awesome and confusing at the same time. My body buzzed like I was being charged by some sort of electrical device. I had never felt anything like it before and the energy was extremely disruptive. The only thing I can compare it to is a sexual energy that simply intruded and persisted, leaving me with a primal, wanton energy that was off the charts! It was way worse than wanting to be with a man. There was no logic to it, and I was left feeling confused and powerless.

"The next thing that happened frightened me even more. Someone unseen instructed me to lie down on the bed after a session. It is my understanding that the intention was to release the pent up energy through the crown but it hadn't happened that way. What I felt was an utterly raw, primitive sexual energy and extremely disturbing. The result was, for me, completely and utterly devastating. At that point, I felt incapable to make mentally sound choices—to think coherently. Needless to say, I was very frightened and angry! To need to release the energy became my top priority—my entire focus. I became irrational…no longer able to sort things through." I stopped speaking as the most prominent images of the event lingered to play havoc in my mind.

"Quem?"

"Yes, Dear One."

"I really don't wish to keep writing about this. I do not want to think of it! What happened next was shocking and for me was way beyond anything I considered to be acceptable. Besides, Quem, seriously, this is absolutely no one's business!"

Once again Quem encouraged me, "Nakala, I ask you to continue. There are others who would benefit from this knowledge."

I sucked in a deep breath before I went on. "Well, honestly, at that point I thought I had lost it. A spiritual being came to me and made me feel like I was having a sexual encounter with a man. Quite literally, I felt the energy and the intention. Even so there was no relief from the energy. It was then that I begged for protection, mercy, and for that horrifying nightmare to end.

"I have only heard about this type of encounter two other times. One was in a fiction novel. The second time, I was actually seeking help from an individual and was explaining what happened in as few words as possible. I had been so embarrassed and ashamed. I really thought I had done something wrong—that I had caused the entire thing out of my stupidity!

"This person that I had confided to explained that they thought it had been a spiritual rape because it had been against my will. I had to agree because I didn't know any better and I still don't. I did not ask for any of that to happen.

"The entire experience was odd because the energy came on at night more than any other time. But there at the end the energy consumed me like a raging fire. I was feeling this energy in my genital area that felt invasive to the point of being painful. I really don't know how to describe the energy other than it was a strong tingling sensation, a vibration. Try that for a few hours and see where it gets you! The energy was uncomfortable in the extreme and felt wrong! I wanted, no, needed, it to stop! By then, I was literally close to losing my sanity. I questioned where the energy came from. The energy consumed me. I could not sleep. I tried to distract myself. I crossed my legs. I tried to run! I recited nursery rhymes, I sang songs and I called people on the phone. Nothing worked! What I felt was horrible and I couldn't escape it. I finally told Scott in as few words as possible what I was feeling. (This was before I had told him I wanted a divorce.) I went to him out of shear desperation. I had to do something, try anything! I went to him for support—protection, even. Although I knew he would not understand or be able to do anything, just having him near gave me some comfort. I knew what he thought (crazy). However, he didn't saying anything condescending.

"My understanding was that I was being controlled by earth-bound spirits or some sort of evil entities. Their sole purpose, I had believed, was that they were quite literally working to drive me crazy. Quem, is this true?"

"Nakala," Quem explained, "What was happening was an initiation to bring forth the awakening of the kundalini."

"Quem," I countered, "At the time I didn't even know what that meant! I am still not for sure what the kundalini stuff is all about. At the time that this happened, I was in a very confused state of mind. None of the beings who were working with me explained anything! Quite literally I began to worry about my mental state. I strongly suspected that I was on the verge of a mental breakdown. How long could I go without sleep and have this type of energy invade my body? I felt desperate and my life was quickly spiraling out of control. Why was this allowed to happen?"

"In answer to your question," Quem began, "there are masters, many; they all have a particular style to their teaching. You had been taught that you could communicate by asking what was happening. Yet you didn't. It was done in an extreme manner, I agree. The teachings were accelerated for you, Nakala. I know the overall experience was painful, and through it all you initiated the end of your marriage of thirty-five years. But know that this piece of it—the separation and ultimate divorce was the design to your purpose. There is a great shift occurring and you are to be up and running for your part in future events."

My mind began to sort through the pieces of information until they fit together in a pattern that somewhat retained clarity and logic. With an indescribable swiftness I realized that Quem was my Master and it was He who had put forth the over-all plan. Then my emotions took charge: I was stunned and in an accusatory tone I blurted out, "Oh, my God… You?" My mouth dropped open unable to find my voice—wanting to disbelieve—for someone to refute my dreadful conclusion.

As I thought over the ramifications, I felt my constitution soften a bit and stated. "You are my Master, Quem. You are the one who accelerated my teachings?"

"Yes!" His response was quick, strong, and sure! His tone had an unmistakable measure of warning that I worked to disregard, "You know not what comes down the pike!"

"Quem, I was so embarrassed and ashamed. I didn't know who to turn to. I literally thought I was going crazy. Nathanal, what about Nathanal? He was there the entire time?"

"Nakala," Quem stoically assured me, "his purpose was to sit with it… remain completely unattached to what was happening."

Incredulously, I countered, "Quem, is that even possible?"

The conversation I had with Nathanal just days before about feeling each other's emotions was all I could think of. In dismay, I cried out, "He could see what was happening and could feel my pain…all of it? All of the time you both knew how desperate I was; yet you did nothing? I thought quite literally that if I didn't get help, I would die."

"Nakala," Quem began to explain in a soothing tone, "We knew what we were doing. Yes, it was extreme to say the least, but you made it. As I said earlier, your teachings were and continue to be speed up—escalated."

I had to stop. No longer could I speak. Quem had left nothing in the shadows for me to assume. He had clearly outlined that my teachings were accelerated and now he is saying they will continue to be accelerated. "Why Quem?" was all I could get out.

Slowly with deliberation Quem repeated himself, "As I said, we had to get you ready for what was to come your way. Know that the lessons continue, Nakala."

"Oh God," I muttered, a bit disoriented and disillusioned, "What more can I handle? Quem, will you please explain to me your reasons…I mean what was it that was so important that you had to put me through such a horrible ordeal?"

"First off, Dear One, the worst is out of the way. Nakala, know that there are a multitude of reasons. You are being prepared for grand. You are my daughter, Nakala. There is much I am to teach you in a precise period of time. Know that there are a host of beings who surround you and are supporting you with love to ease you through this transition. The initiations are many that come your way. It was never my aim to place you in harm's way. Your Higher Self is in direct communications with us: your Pleiadian family and others who have come to your aid."

"You are in communication with my Higher Self? What about my I AM Presence?"

Again Quem channeled a deep and relaxing breath through me. I felt myself surrender before Quem took up the conversation once again. "These are one and the same, Nakala. I use the terminology interchangeably.

"Nakala, it is time you took a rest from the writing. Rise and move about." I sighed, agreeing with his suggestion. He knew best. But before I got up from my desk I asked, "Will you work with me later when I return?" "Yes, my young daughter. After you have rested for a time come back and we will resume."

CHAPTER
ELEVEN

For the last several hours I had been receiving and typing telepathic communications and to finally hear Quem say that I should go take some time to move was so very much appreciated. I itched to get up to do something physical. Thinking about all that Quem had said…well I wanted to get away from it and allow it all to steep and just sit with it to process at its own volition.

Earlier I had noticed that the flowerbeds could sure use some clean-up. But instead I decided to tackle the chore of washing the patio sliding doors. For a few weeks now I had looked at the spots on them thinking that I'd get to it soon. Oh, there is that eternal word again: soon. As I thought about the word "soon" I remembered how many times my guides had spoken that word and laughed. Finally, things in my life had aligned for me to have the correct set of circumstances to wash the patio doors!

Promptly, I gathered my supplies and went after the task. However, while I washed the glass, the words of my husband's response to my confession began to replay themselves. Boldly, I had met his accusing stare and stated, "I can't communicate with you any longer."

He had taken the defensive and reacted saying, "Well, as long as we are being honest…" He had paused, momentarily weighing his words before he had shrewdly added, "I think you should go see someone—get your head x-rayed." He had gone on to say something about a CT for the brain, but I had been far away by that time.

In that instant, his words had blazed through my mind, giving me a candid overview of what had occurred between the two of us. Swiftly, without wavering, I had gathered more than enough momentum to take me all the way to the finish line. For me there had been nothing left to fight for. Finally I knew I was finished with the marriage…with him. After his last statement, for me there was not a single moment of looking back. Not once. I was amazed at how easily it had been for me to walk away from all of those years—all those memories.

A little over a year later, our divorce was finalized on the very day of our thirty-fifth wedding anniversary. Some would call it kismet. I found it to be ironic to the point of being painful.

During the divorce proceedings there hadn't been any of the usual nasty negotiations that are so famous for couples in the midst of a divorce. Even so, there had been a few friends who advised me to use a "cooling off period". However, my emotions had taken over; I had wanted out as quickly as possible.

On occasion there had been others—my attorney for one—who had bluntly warned that Scott would take me to the proverbial cleaners. They all had been wrong. Scott had offered a more than fair settlement. I had gratefully accepted.

During our court appearance the judge had openly applauded our ability to work with each other peacefully. Afterwards, I sank back with the stark realization that my life would never be the same…I didn't *want* it to ever be the same!

✳ ✳ ✳

Major life changes like a death in the family, relocation, career shifts, and divorces are said to be the most stressful times in one's life, often leading people indiscriminately into the murky depths of depression. Fortunately for me I didn't have any of that. Maintaining my property kept me extremely active with no time to dwell on being alone—on my own. I decided to put my home up for sale. The size and mortgage were much too large. I was counting on a quick sale. Immediately, I put my attention on repairs to the interior of the house for maximum show-appeal.

Ironically, the repairs began the same month I was notified of my father's hospitalization. Diabetes had gotten completely out of control, and after an initial consultation, the doctors made the disclosure that they suspected that he was suffering from dementia as well. As Power of Attorney, my physical presence had been expected. Soon the hospital would hand him off to a rehabilitation facility to be stabilized and to complete the evaluation. The staff at the hospital told me, "He will require constant care at least for the next several weeks."

Immediately I saw that he could no longer care for himself. Earlier I had witnessed times of confusion, but had no idea what the cause had been. I had noticed that his talk had become grandiose to the point of being egotistical. He bragged about his accumulated wealth, which I knew nothing about. After a while, I began to question where he had been coming up with this. As far as I knew he didn't have that kind of money. But I kept my mouth shut and continued to come and visit him as often as I could.

After his hospitalization I went to his home and saw the clutter, the filth that he had created. I saw various pieces of mail scattered about. I saw mice and lots of them!

As I looked closer I found various documents indicating his actions. He had been writing checks for cash. I could only surmise from what he had been saying that he was giving the money away. (He had been wealthy. Why not?) He had not written any of the amounts down in his check ledger. So I played like a detective and looked through stacks of papers and photos, under the cushions, and behind and under furniture for bank statements.

During that time I asked myself some really difficult questions. 'Could he go home and be safe? Should I move in with him? Could I depend on well-meaning friends who offered to come by and give him his insulin shots and check up on him? Should he be placed in assisted living or a nursing home?' These were all questions that had to be answered for our highest good as a family.

Soon it became evident that he required full-time, dependable care.

During this time I was spread thin, seeing to my father's affairs, repairing my own home to place on the market, and now I had begun to clean my father's home, preparing for either his return or possibly in preparation to sell. This all happened in the month of July, the hottest month of the year for Kansas. My father didn't have air conditioning. *Could it get any worse, I wondered?*

Every other week, I drove to Wichita to work at my father's house and see to his care. All the while I continued my work with the Ascended Masters by doing channeled readings and the daily dictations. I only had recently begun to feel comfortable working with several guides, Nathanal, Benjamin, and Tulró. On top of it all, my first book, *When Angels Speak,* was due to be published. I had landed in a precarious position. I was maxed out, physically, mentally and emotionally.

A wave of love came over me and I knew that I had company. *But who?*

"Nakala, sit a moment with me." Quem began. So I just sat there and allowed his love to wash away all of my feelings of fatigue and doubt that I could take care of what was before me.

After several minutes, Quem said, "Let us set our attention to your immediate future. There is much that you are about to encounter. Your father on the Earth plane is ill and requires attention. You are to see to it that he receives the care that is necessary to make him comfortable and safe. No longer is he able to see to himself. Rid yourself of thoughts and feelings of guilt that are derived from the belief that, as the only child left, it is your responsibility to physically nurse him. Nakala, you are not to see to him personally as you are of the stature petite. He is a large man with needs that exceed your ability to give.

"At this time you are to see to his financial affairs, including his real estate. This for you is quite enough to add to your responsibilities. We will see to it that he obtains what he requires."

Suddenly, I saw more of the picture and felt the weight of it all take me down once again. I knew that Quem was correct. I also knew it hadn't been Quem's intention to bring forth any negativity on my part, but I feared for my father's mental, emotional, physical, and spiritual state. I loved him.

I had seen what these sort of places could do to a person's will—how they could break the spirit. How will he fare to be housed simply in wait for the inevitable? Never did I want it to come to this…to put him in a nursing facility away from his home, friends, and family.

Then I felt my heart expand with encouragement. My view shifted and a peace overtook me. In case he didn't come home, there were nursing facilities that were cheerful, with staff that loved the residents. I prayed if it came to that, I would find the perfect place for my father. I knew Quem was correct. I would not be able to care for him…not on a physical level.

"Nakala I give you this. Your home is up for sale and soon you will be moving to be near your parents. The three-hour drive you are making to see to their needs is wearing on you. We desire you to be settled in one place. You are to follow your heart in this matter. They are both nearing their transition soon. So you are to find a place suitable to your needs and ready yourself for the move."

I swallowed hard, knowing this had been coming. I immediately began to go over my mental list of things that had to be finished before I could pack my household and personal belongings and go. Then I heard Quem say, "Your Nathanal will see to the details concerning all. He is guiding you, Nakala. Allow him this."

CHAPTER
TWELVE

I wondered if it could get any worse. My belief was, yes, it could. When I acknowledged that my father wasn't coming home, ever, I knew that I had to do something with Mr. Wrinkles, my father's dog. Mr. Wrinkles, an elderly golden lab, to my dismay, had lived in a fenced-in yard that couldn't hold him. Because of this he had been chained to a tree for many years. It hadn't been out of meanness that this had happened.

The dog had easy access to the garage, food, and water. My father loved that dog; and, in the beginning, had diligently trained him to sit, stay, roll over, pee on demand (I am not kidding here), and get in the bed of his red pickup truck and ride all over town. Mr. Wrinkles would obediently stay in the truck while my father went in to have coffee with his friends and do other errands around town. Mr. Wrinkles had learned many commands and my father was proud of him. Mr. Wrinkles had been allowed to come indoors on occasion when the weather turned cold. Mr. Wrinkles weighed close to eighty pounds.

Now, suddenly, Mr. Wrinkles had become my responsibility and, for me, was unmanageable. Mr. Wrinkles either was too old, had forgotten how to obey, or possibly he just hadn't gotten comfortable with me. Every time I went to see to him, he tried to jump on me and the weight behind him nearly knocked me down as his nails dug into my skin. I couldn't get him to do anything.

For three weeks I stewed over the enormity of my situation. I questioned how I could possibly find a good home for him. Taking note the dog was old, had never been neutered, was bull-headed, liked to roam, and was physically powerful, I felt my options were limited. I simply didn't have high hopes for his placement. Most people were not in the market for this type of dog.

After talking to different people around our small town and placing ads, with no response, I called all of the no-kill facilities in the area, leaving me only more discouraged. The facilities were all at full capacity. I was at the end of my rope with no more ideas on how to continue to care for him. The weather had been well over 100 degrees for weeks now. It was simply abusive to leave Mr. Wrinkles in this weather while depending on the neighbors and friends to take care of him in my absence. I constantly worried that someone would forget to come give him fresh water and food. I had to find this dog a home and fast.

Finally, I made the decision that I would take him to the humane society the next day. In my defense, I felt I had no choice. Leaving Mr. Wrinkles unattended in this heat with only an occasional visit from the neighbors was irresponsible on my part. That is when I heard Nathanal say, wait until tomorrow. So I did.

The very next day I was standing in my father's front yard with the insurance adjuster discussing the hail-damaged roof when I noticed an individual slowly driving an extended cab truck down the quiet neighborhood street as if he was patrolling the area. The white truck caught and held my attention because it was out of place—conspicuous even— because not only was it quite large and super-clean but the truck had been detailed with red, orange, and yellow flames shooting down the sides.

As if I were magnetized to the scene, I followed the movement of the truck as it slowed down even more in front of my father's house and turned to pull into the drive. Curious, I stepped away from the adjuster (he was preparing to climb on the roof anyway), and walked toward the older man who had opened the truck door preparing to step out. He stuck his hand out and said, "Hello, I am Mike McFarland. You must be Bill's daughter?" As I took his hand in mine I felt something familiar take hold. He continued his introduction. "I know your father."

Respectfully, I commented on his truck—how beautiful it was and that I admired the detail. As Mike revealed more about himself, all of the pieces began to fall into place. My father and Mike had both owned their own body shops—did their own paint and detailing jobs—they were good friends.

Then Mike asked, "How is your dad?" Not waiting for my answer, he began to lay out why he was there. "I heard that he is in the nursing home in Halstead." I nearly choked as my answer caught in my throat. "Yes, and I don't think he is going to come home."

Unexpectedly, Mike revealed, "Well, I always told your dad that if anything ever happened to him, I would take Mr. Wrinkles." I gasped at his words, not daring to speak. Self-consciously, I brushed away a tear that had slipped down my cheek. *Had I heard him correctly? Could he be serious?* As if it were an everyday occurrence, Mike went on to say, "I'll come by tomorrow and pick him up."

The next day I kept busy by going through another pile of clothes and "treasures" that my father had accrued over the last few years. There were boxes and stacks of stuff everywhere. The mice that I had mentioned earlier had gotten into everything, creating probably the worst mess I ever had to deal with. That in itself gave me pause.

I had just decided to begin pulling up the old olive green carpet that I knew to be thirty-five years old. The sweat dripped down my back and in between my breasts. I had to keep blowing my nose to get the dirt out of it. I found myself constantly looking at the clock wondering where Mike was. As it neared 4:30 PM, Mike had still not shown up. The pressure of disappointment was so incredible that it bordered on depression. *Why hadn't he come by?* However, I kept at my task digging in harder. The dirt that flew off the carpet stuck to my sweaty skin. No matter, I told myself, being pretty then wasn't important.

At 5:10 I heard a knock on the door and saw it was Mike. Sure enough, Mike had kept his word. I had not taken into account that he still ran a business. Inviting Mike in, I saw that he carried a leash and a large dog biscuit. Umm, he came well prepared.

Not delaying our chore, we walked out back to get Mr. Wrinkles and took him to the truck. When Mike opened the cab door for Mr. Wrinkles to get in, I sucked in a deep breath. I stood there in disbelief and began to fidget as I questioned Mike's choice. Mr. Wrinkles was filthy: the loose hairs and dust were flying off of his coat. I stood there in disbelief as I couldn't fathom Mike's action. *Wasn't Mike going to put the dog in the bed of the truck?* I looked inside the cab and saw it was brand spanking new…not a speck of dust anywhere—nothing out of place. *OMG! The dog would shred the seats in no time.*

This time, I took Mike's arm to get his attention and asked, "Mike are you sure? Mr. Wrinkles…" I heard my voice begin to trail off, "is so… dirty." Mike gave a hearty laugh and smiled. Lovingly, Mike turned his full attention to Mr. Wrinkles, patted the seat, and with a reassuring voice prompted the dog, "Mr. Wrinkles how about you and I go for a ride?" Mr. Wrinkles pumped his tail with enthusiasm and made the jump. However, he missed. Seeing the dog's nails scrap the tan leather upholstery, I grimaced and looked away. Mike's truck had been flawless, yet Mike kept an even tone and again encouraged Mr. Wrinkles to give it another go. This time, however, Mike gave him a forceful shove from behind. Did I mention that Mr. Wrinkles slobbers?

So this is why Nathanal had asked me to wait another day. I didn't know how this event had been orchestrated, only that one of my prayers had been answered. Somehow they had lined up everything so that Mr. Wrinkles could have a new home where he would be loved.

CHAPTER
THIRTEEN

Just as I finished typing the above paragraph I heard someone telepathically say a word that I was not familiar with. *Was it a name?* Writing about my father and his dog had brought up a gamut of emotions…grief…gratitude; and I had been trying with all of my might not to cry. Just when I was about to give up and let loose my pent up emotion, I heard the word repeated. Deciding that it must be a name, I got my journal to write it down. It sounded like Casmar; but after hearing it a couple more times, I wrote down Kazmar. Evidently, this *person* wanted to speak to me, so I sat with it and allowed him to talk. He said he was from Venus. Unusual, I thought, as most of *my* visitors are from Pleiades or Sirius.

From habit, I asked if he wanted me to create a journal for his messages. Without hesitation he answered, "No." So instead I grabbed my personal journal and wrote down the date, time, and location of the transmission. Then as I wrote down his name, Kazmar, I asked if the spelling were correct. "Yes," he answered.

Making small talk, Kazmar casually complimented me on the pictures throughout my home of the Masters, Jesus, El Morya, Germain, Mother Mary, and various others that hung on the walls and sat on small tables. I felt my vibration rise when he said, "I see the display of pictures of masters about of those you appeal to for assistance in manner all." To elaborate he added, "What I say is there are many who wish to communicate with beings such as you."

Not knowing exactly what Kazmar meant, I overlooked his comment and moved on to ask, "Are you a fifth dimensional being?" Not directly answering my question he answered, "I am of a higher sector, yes. I am a being that is considered to be of the Light. I ask you, why do you ask questions such as these?"

"Well," I answered, "I am asking questions so I may learn about you. I do not readily know why you have come to speak to me. What is your purpose?"

"You write the books. Many of us see what you do. There are those such as myself who desire to assist you in the telling of the stories."

At that point I was genuinely baffled. Babaró and Samuel Paul were generally the ones who directed me with the writings. Babaró is currently the head writer of *The Accounts of a Pleiadian Traveler* series and presumably he must approve all material. So what happens when others stop by and offer their assistance? Personally, I cannot do anything. I certainly cannot just say, "Okay, Kazmar let's sit down and see what you can do." But then in a flash, I reassessed the dilemma and asked myself, "Maybe I could?"

In the background, I heard someone make a sound like he was clearing his throat exclusively to catch my attention. I suspected it might be Babaró.

"Yes, indeed," Babaró declared. "You have looked beyond the perimeters known to you that have been arranged by the Comterous. (Comterous is a Pleiadian group formed for the purpose of inspiring certain works in the fields of literature and the mass media technologies, which include but are not limited to radio, recorded music, film and television.)

Babaró encouraged me by saying, "Dear, Nakala, in all situations, be they connected to your writings or not, it is good to ask what is for the highest good of all concerned. Perhaps you ask Kazmar to put together a presentation of his qualifications and his intent. I believe this request to be in order."

Kazmar channeled a movement through me taking me completely by surprise. He took my fist and thumped it twice on my chest then lifted that same fist high in the air and shook it as if he had achieved something of great worth! As he channeled these movements, I felt a strong sense that he had been empowered by Babaró's optimistic view.

Never had I asked for a résumé from any of the spiritual writers that I channel—I had never even considered the idea! I mean seriously? Always, I had worked with the same group who had worked with and through me from the very beginning.

Oh, there were others who came by, but generally the beings who guided me through the writing process had been teaching me through different forms of communication for some time. I had had plenty of time to develop a steadfast relationship with them.

This Kazmar person was another story altogether. He just showed up out of nowhere and indicated that he wanted to assist me. Okay....

Honestly, I doubted that I could conduct an in-depth interview with a Being of Light. Generally, during sessions with humans, it is better to have them physically sitting before me in person or at the very least have a phone conference. (With telepathic communications I have noticed there are times I am unable to pick up on subtle nuances.) I thought in order to get a better sense of clients' characters and qualifications it is a smarter choice to talk to them in person. Definitely, I would consider things like how they held their body: were they relaxed? Did they make eye contact? And, in general, I would observe how well they were able to articulate their desires, abilities, and even their own requirements. I had no way to observe people if I could not see them.

But really, as I thought on my quandary, was it necessary at all that Kazmar command a particular presence or have social skills?

I did believe, however, that he must be honest, reliable, and exhibit a certain character in order to work with me. In addition, he required the ability to write well—with style and finesse—for story telling that would captivate our designated audience.

Enthralled, I felt the endeavor worthy of giving it the ol' college try and went on to ask, "Well, Kazmar what do you think?" Suddenly, my body sat straight as a ramrod—rigid. Instantly, I was directed to look at the vision board I had tacked on the wall behind my computer. (The vision board was covered with words and pictures that I had picked out that reflected my desires.) My eyes were directed and locked onto, first, the words 'breathe easy' until I had read it making a mental connection. Next, I was guided to look at the word, 'recreation'. Oh, I had his attention all right and from what he had directed me to see, I concluded that he had assessed the opportunity and thought it would be a piece of cake…a vacation and, of course, fun!

I am well aware that the masters and some guides are able to channel movements through people. At least I have known a few people who have encountered things such as this, thus relieving me somewhat of my own personal anxieties concerning the phenomenon. But for a being that I have never worked with before…to be able to channel movements through me gave me reason to pause and ask, "How do they do it?" On a number of occasions I have asked this question with the answer always being the same, "energy." Is the same technique used with channeling thoughts and words through a person? How is it all accomplished? If Beings of Light can do this, then why can't an accomplished person in a physical body who is high vibrational do the same thing?

Feeling a shift in vibration, I wondered if Babaró had decided to comment on my question. Nothing happened for a few minutes, which made me feel a little uneasy. Maybe it was just too complicated for me to understand let alone write about! I decided to take another approach and ask the question again, thinking I may possibly have moved to another level and now was ready for a more in-depth explanation of how movements are channeled.

"Babaró," I began in a hopeful tone, knowing full well he knew that I wanted a complete answer that I could understand, "Could you please explain to me how you channel your messages and movements through me?"

"Nakala, of course I *can* explain to you how I channel through you. And I believe that it is time that you receive an appropriate answer that is expanded. You have shown yourself as ready for this teaching. I am able to communicate with you telepathically from anywhere and I do! But for the most part I am in your aura directly sending commands, projecting ideas, thought forms, images, and feeling. I may choose from a variety of methods of communication I desire to give through you."

"You are saying that you are outside of my physical body?" I did not wait for Babaró to respond. Instead I was thinking of a comment someone had said in my presence about us being like puppets on strings and said, "Sounds a bit like I am a robot and you hold a remote control."

I thought that possibly these beings had joined my physical body somehow. Vividly, I remembered during the most intense time of my attunements with my spiritual gifts, I saw with my third eye a being bending down to align his self with my body and merge into it. Distinctly, I had felt the energy of that being enter my body. So that experience brought up another question.

"Ah, yes! Well, there are different levels of the merging of two or more entities."

"Yes," I said, "'two or more' as this merge may involve one to several individuals or a group consciousness."

"Honey, yes there are those who join with the physical body—yours. Literally there are two or more consciousness's sharing the same body. In this case yours, usually there is no indication—no outer sign that this is occurring.

"Because you have become more consciously aware that we use several methods to communicate with you and others, you are experiencing more and more of our Union." I paused in wonder at the complexity and implications of his words.

"Nakala, just type my words and you will come to understand. Your question is complex, having multifaceted answers as there are different areas of expertise and levels of understanding and skill. When you qualify for a more involved teaching then certainly you will receive it!

"There are beings with different abilities and different purposes or specialties. We explain that there are those who reside in the spirit realm such as your Stephanó who is master/doctor/surgeon. He introduced himself to you in the early days as such and has given you countless teachings. Stephanó is an Ascended Master of the Pleiades Nation and meticulously delves into many areas such as scientific research, astrology, psychology, the arts; and overall he is passionate in the studies of the human condition.

"Stephanó works as a medical doctor to ease physical maladies and all the while studies the cause for them…to get to the core issue that has caused them. Example: you have self-worth issues. I'll add here, who doesn't? This is truth. But to get to the individual core issue we must get to the root of the manifestation of your physical issue. I dare say that you have had multitudes of embodiments and life experiences that have left you on the road of blind limitation concerning particular beliefs. Those beliefs conclusively do not serve you for your highest good. Meaning there are experiences that have taken you off track away from the Light of God." I hesitated, not understanding exactly what Babaró had meant. Before I had a chance to ask him to clarify, Babaró asked, "Right there I lost you, didn't I Nakala?"

"Yep, what you said…some of my experiences took me away from the Light of God. Well, I didn't quite get it. You are saying that something I did took me away from the Light of God?"

"Light of God is another way of saying God's Love, Nakala. That is all."

I felt I understood and replied, "Oh, I get it. But what happened to my question?"

Babaró's energy had shifted. I felt it more intensely as if he had acquired a greater momentum or focus to his teaching. In other words, he had gone into high gear and I felt it energetically!

"I wanted to give you some background on who and why (the criteria) particular Beings of Light will merge their consciousness with someone like you who is residing in a physical body. Know this: you are assessed before any beings are allowed to come into your field—before they commence to guide and or communicate with you. We are your Pleiadian family: we watch over you closely and always, to a certain degree, we have been allowed to guide and protect you!

"To be crystal clear, when I say, 'someone like you,' I refer to what you have evolved as: your personality, your attributes, abilities, and your openness to love and be loved—your devotion to God. In other words, how awake you are to God's Love. Also, your tendencies are considered as well. Are you asking, allowing, and accepting assistance from those of the higher realms?

"Stephanó is a Master Teacher who has ascended from the dense energies of the physical world. This gives him a higher more expanded perspective of the human condition as well as the ability to control his energy. He learned from his experiences on Earth what works best for him as he goes about with communications to assist with not only people like you but with all beings! Stephanó is fully capable of merging his consciousness with yours and does so by communicating with you telepathically.

He does this by directing his thought (very focused) and feeling to you. He merges with your energetic or etheric body.

"I do the same. However, I am not an ascended master like your Stephanó."

Babaró paused long enough for me to review his statements and formulate any questions if I desired. "So Babaró, you are saying that even unascended beings may have the ability to communicate with people in physical bodies."

"Yes, look at people who have passed on like your great aunt did recently. She did not have the background or teachings that expanded her awareness in the area of the metaphysical. However, when she passed from her physical body she was fully capable of communicating with you! You see?"

"Well, Babaró, I sort of understand. My aunt, she never channeled through me though. She only briefly communicated with me after her transition."

Babaró, working to make sure I understood his explanation, continued, "Still, Nakala, she was able to telepathically (through the mind) exchange information. After you leave the dense physical body the barriers are dropped. At that time, she had not had the level of awareness that she could channel through you messages or movements."

"Okay, you are saying that this is a learned thing…to channel through a person thoughts, feelings, movements, and so on?"

"Very much so, Nakala. It takes expertise to do what we do."

PART
FIVE

TELEPATHIC COMMUNICATIONS

CHAPTER

FOURTEEN

After my conversation with Babaró about channeling energy through another person, I wondered even more about it all.

For the premise—all rational—I had decided to approach a friend, who is really more like a sister, Crystal, who lived out of state. We talked on the phone at least once a week. I figured that if I worked with her by sending her thoughts (images or words) just prior to our phone conversations, she would eventually get them. She could do the same. We both tried sending and receiving. It all seemed logical to me.

The two of us had a close connection and I didn't figure that the span of miles would make any difference. We worked on it for about three weeks before we lost interest in the exercise. We had never had what I would call a *hit*. I could feel her love (I thought), but maybe I had been feeling my own. It could have been that we didn't try for a long enough period of time, or perhaps we just didn't know the correct protocol in order to telepathically communicate.

We both were working with our guides, the ascended masters, and the angelic realm; and well, it all just seemed like it *should* work. I reasoned if I can converse with the higher realms like this, why couldn't I converse with someone on the physical as well? What was the problem? I have asked for guidance concerning it all. What do I do?

At once I felt my vibration rise and heard Babaró say, "Nakala dearest, do not fret over this. You are being guided in all manner and receive the gifts as you are intended to. Do you remember when you first worked with the pendulum? How incredibly focused you had been on achieving? It is the same with anything. Continue to practice your telepathic communications with Crystal. Choose a time and stick with it. You are training the mind—programming it to your will. Your intent must be programmed and run regularly. This means practice every day. Soon you will begin to see that you are sending and receiving the correct information.

"I caution you: Keep it simple. Use one object at a time—one word— think the word and send the image as well. Keep at it! Soon you will reap the rewards."

"Ah, Babaró, I see you have chosen to use the eternal word, *soon.*" I chuckled to myself as I thought on it.

Babaró didn't even crack a smile, but instead decided to remain on track with his teaching, "Yes, it is a matter of your thought and feeling, how much you desire to achieve…how much energy you are willing to put forth to the endeavor is a direct connection as to *when* you receive the gift."

Not completely satisfied I asked another question, "Babaró, is it really that much different…?" However, before I had finished my question my thoughts shifted as I thought I already understood the answer, but I decided to ask anyway. "What I mean to ask is…is communicating with you telepathically so much different than with a person who is residing in the physical?"

"Yes!" Babaró stated quickly. "Our abilities exceed. Listen Nakala, we are trained, but there is more to this. We are of the higher realms. Energy is. There is nothing of the lower denser energies that impede us in our communications with you. We are of the Light!"

Babaró paused to allow me to reflect on his statement before he pressed on. "You are in the physical realm. The energy in this realm is of a slow sort and so much of the time is misqualified: meaning you are not at the level to *believe* that *anything* is possible. You still swim in an ocean of mistruths. Do not despair over my words, Nakala! You are making progress. Your desire must be great—strong—unwavering to learn and practice the ways of the Ascended Host!"

"So Babaró, you are saying just stay with it? Work with Crystal by sending the thoughts and the images to her?"

However, before Babaró had the opportunity to answer me, I had formulated another question. "Wait, Babaró, thought is the intention but feeling is the power behind the thought. What feeling should I be creating?"

"Nakala, dear one, for now just concentrate on the word and image when you are sending. Clear the mind before you desire to receive from your friend. For now, follow these directives."

"Okay, sounds simple enough."

"Remember if you desire to achieve quickly, keep at it!"

Evidently Babaró thought we had talked long enough on how to begin to receive telepathic communications as he swiftly shifted the subject. "You have inadvertently looked over something of significant importance. When you desire anything you are creating thought and emotion before it comes into your reality, no matter what it is! In order to receive, you must stay focused on it! My example is your desire to bring in or magnetically draw into your life a housemate…a husband. (Remember like attracts like.) But I say to you oft times you desire such as a husband, because it is your ego that wants attention. It is these times the Higher Self is not directing you…it is your Ego! Perhaps it is not in alignment to have a relationship just yet. In other words, you are not ready for the experience on the level your Higher Self desires. Your Higher Self is running the show unless your Ego takes command. Only when the Higher Self is ready to express itself in this manner through the human vehicle will you be presented with the appropriate candidate. You will know for certain the man is the perfect choice by the way you feel in your heart (promptings from the Great I AM (the God in you) or your Higher Self.

"You have two forces at play here: the Higher Self and the Ego (your personality or lower consciousness). You, as a collective consciousness, have been trained well by the ego to depend on outside stimuli to keep you in a place of superficial happiness which is a shallow formulation and a destructive one, at that, of your true essence. It all feels fine and acceptable until the stimuli have ceased. This is all an illusion. In order for you to continue in this state your ego must continue to receive data via communications from others or yourself, telling you that you are worthy—but only as long as you continue to receive said data or, in this case, a relationship with a male partner.

"Because you have been in a relationship for so many years, you have presented an image or status to the outer world and even to yourself that you are of the sector who have attained…is good enough to have and continue to have. Even if the marriage wasn't aligned with God's Will, what I say is truth.

"Currently your ego flares at the thought of not having. It desires the affirmation that you are indeed worthy to have and hold a man of good standing.

"If you do not have a man on your arm, your ego becomes disenchanted and tricks you into thinking you are not good enough—not worthy.

"So it goes from there; you begin to put out thoughts and feelings that you want a mate. The only thing is, you have not healed from the last relationship.

"I say your ego has grown accustomed to having a male companion in the home, and to shift this belief takes a bit of doing. No matter that the relationship wasn't the best. You still are striving to achieve this type of energy. Your ego wants you to believe that, unless you have a mate, there is something wrong with you. So you continue to create energetic signals, if you will, of desire and so on until someone picks up on this energy. In essence, to feel worthy you look for ways in order to boost your self-confidence. You have become dependent on receiving attention from outside sources even if it is negative. Because of your social programing (your belief system), it is your belief to feel complete (worthy, lovable, whole, good enough), you must have man on arm."

"You know Babaró, that I have met this guy, Sam, through a friend I have in the master gardener program, right?"

"Nakala there is nothing that goes unnoticed by us. Why is it that you think I brought this subject up?"

"Oh," I said as I felt my face redden with embarrassment. "Well, I brought it up, Babaró because well…I don't know why he just appeared like he did. My friend, who actually was my mentor in the program, introduced us. To be quite honest, I am pretty sure she was just trying to ditch him. She thought of me because this fellow is into reflexology, massage, and Reiki energy work. Of course, I am interested because my desire is to meet someone, specifically of the male gender, who is interested in the same things I am!

"He wants to go out with me…go to a movie and dinner. I agreed because I would really like to go out! Just have a little fun. However, his energy is rather intense. He is a big man…not overweight, really, but tall and muscular and seems like he may be depressed or something. I am unable to figure him out."

"Nakala this would be a wonderful opportunity to do a spiritual reading. He would be a most willing participant. Ask him if he would allow."

"Wow, Babaró I am surprised you suggested that I do a reading for this man."

"Nakala he will be a most willing and agreeable subject for you. He is well aware of the higher realms and who resides therein. Simply tell him that your guides want you to do this for him."

"Yes, okay, I'll ask him what he thinks when I meet him for the movie."

Suddenly, I just had to be honest with Babaró and said, "Oh God, I have a headache that just will not let up. The discomfort is a total distraction from working with you. I want to quit writing for the day."

"Nakala it would do you good to excuse yourself for a few moments and do the following: Get some water and hydrate yourself—a tall glass—see if that doesn't alleviate the discomfort."

I did as he recommended, but it didn't seem to help. Maybe in a few minutes the pain would be gone or at least subside. So I just sat in my swivel rocker with my eyes closed for a while. Still my head throbbed. I know there are techniques (several) to take care of this but for some reason I was unable to concentrate well enough to remember any of them.

I felt a deep breath channeled through me then heard Babaró say, "Nakala, I offer up the suggestion because people of the earth often do not hydrate themselves properly. When you have an ache or pain, it is because there is a block in the energy flow. Since you are mostly made of water you must keep yourself well hydrated. Water is a conductor of energy. In order for the energy of your body to flow properly (operate) you must have the adequate amount of fluid absorbed in the tissue and all therein.

"I continue forth. The energy of the body must be given the correct substance in order to run properly. The breath is vital as well. Breathe in the air while you concentrate on relaxing the body. Perhaps you are tense because of some outer stimuli."

Suddenly, I took my hands and began to massage my temples then the back of my neck. Wow, I noticed the tension and found a not so nice knot that had taken residence at the base of my skull.

"Nakala, the neck massages and the movements that we channeled and continue to channel through you…I would like to expound on the reason for this gift."

"Yes, of course," I answered.

"I remind you," Babaró offered in a soft, sure voice, "They are for reason to enhance the flow of energy. Often tension builds in different areas of the body, depending on the person and reason, and to work the muscles with the breath will assist or perhaps release in entirety the tension. It would be good for you to take heed of my suggestion."

As I began to work the muscles in my neck, I felt Babaró take command of my body and begin to do circular patterns with my head, stretching my neck. I let my arms drop to my sides as he continued. Then he shifted the movement. I decided to follow the pattern that my head was making and could easily see that the movement was in fact an infinity symbol lying on its side. I noticed how good it felt and that my headache had subsided somewhat. After many repetitions Babaró stopped the exercise. I said, "Thank you, Babaró," and suddenly felt a wave of higher energy—the vibration of gratitude—expand outward from my body.

"All that I say with my voice and do through example is for your highest good, Nakala." I noticed that Babaró's tone of voice had become firm as he warned, "However, it is to no avail or purpose if you do not take to heart my advice. The physical body requires attention! The elements are of such import to the physical vehicle that I add them here: air (breath), water (hydration), earth (grounding and the connection with all of God's creation to nourish the physical body, mind, and soul), and fire, (the transmutation of energy and purification by the sacred fires). There is one more—ether (connection to the higher realms of Divine Father-Mother-Creator: *The One*).

"What I have stated in the above paragraph are simply defined and basic concepts, but there is more to the gifts given to you by the elements. Perhaps I shall expand on my teaching as it may be befitting those who desire to understand the nuances of the sacred gifts?

"Take air—to breathe in the element is life itself. When a babe has emerged from his mother's womb, air is given as the first nourishment to the physical body. With air the body flourishes.

"Water—this element, too, is given to sustain and cleanse the physical body. The body cannot survive for more than a few days without this element. Fresh water nourishes the cells allowing them to expand and receive the proper voltage of energy or electricity to serve. Water also purifies the system, flushing out matter of lower, denser vibrations (toxic energy which comes in many forms).

"The element of earth—people require the connection to the Earth's substance—magnetic field. You will notice often with newborns many seem fussy or even colicky (that is what the doctors call it), but it is often a case of the soul being newly embodied but not being grounded. Take the babe and lay him or her on the ground as you stroke his body while speaking or singing softly to him. This being has been out of a physical body for some time and requires the reintroduction to the Earth's magnetic field. You can also hold in your arm, the babe as you sit on the Earth's surface and purposefully connect with the Earth. This means to set your intention of you connecting your body to the Earth.

"You, as well, require connection to the Earth's magnetic field. This means to physically connect with the Earth. To be in nature is so very important for your entire being. For this connection is to assist in the balance of all that you are and desire to become.

"Fire—well misunderstood in your society of today. Fire is the energy of transmutation. You light a fire in your fire place, furnace, or under a pot, and the energy of the fire literally transmutes the cold thus heating your home or food. But fire is so much more! Fire is used in rituals—ceremonies—as sacred rites are being brought forth being set as intention to make promise of what a person or group of persons have set their focus on.

"A flame not unlike any other element has a consciousness and a purpose. Set the purpose or intent and give it to the flame to be carried out by the Divine.

"Today people are being introduced to the Sacred Flames or fire of which each has a specific purpose. There are a multitude of flames, each having a specific color, tone, size and intensity, each to carry forth a specific quality or intention to bring in or amplify more of God's Light.

"Ether—is our last element that I will speak on just now. Ether is what lies beyond your normal third dimensional propensity. The stuff humans generally are unable to see but are most assuredly creating with in every millisecond of their lives with thought and emotion. Ether is what is radiated from the Great Central Sun. Ether is Light substance and what you create with. It is molded into anything and everything in your reality.

"Ether is your connection to the Higher Realms—the Higher Beings of Light. Without Ether there are no transmissions, no communications with beings or intelligences of any sort. In fact there are no beings at all! But it goes beyond this. The earth, flora, and fauna, the starlit skies and the sun of your galaxy are all are created by thought and emotions—molded Light substance or ether!"

"Babaró," I paused for a moment as I reflected on a particular event a few years ago, "I had been outdoors on my patio lying on a lounge chair facing the west. It was evening but there was still plenty of sunshine. I looked up into the sky and saw these tiny particles of light. They almost looked like cells. I had no idea what they were but was enchanted by the sight of them. They seemed to be swimming in the air. The sight reminded me of the cells in blood, how they swim. There had been literally thousands of them. I had asked my guides what they were. The answer I received had been, 'They are tiny bugs.' Because I had no idea what they were, I let it go. But the answer, 'tiny bugs' did not resonate with me at all. Bugs? I mean seriously! Look, Babaró, those little things I saw flitting about in the air, what were they?"

"Ah, Nakala, that what you saw was Light substance. You have the gift, Nakala to see, however, not fully initiated."

"What do you mean I have 'the gift'?"

"I say, Dear One, you have the gift of sight. You can see beyond what people of the "ordinary sector" would consider normal."

Unconvinced, I asked, "So most people aren't able to see the particles?"

"Honey, most people aren't aware Light particles even exist!"

I stopped for a few minutes not sure where to go from here. But then thought, wait a darn minute! "Babaró why did someone…I am not sure which one of my guides told me; it could have been you even, that the Light particles were tiny bugs? Oh my, gosh! Couldn't one of you just tell me the truth? I mean I even asked about the incident afterwards…years after! I wanted a better more complete answer…but really I thought that what I had been told was just plain wrong!"

In a soothing manner Babaró said, "Nakala, calm yourself. One of the facets of this teaching is to trust your intuition."

"Well, Babaró, I did, but where did it get me?"

"Where it got you, Dear One, is that you recognized that there was something incomplete or amiss with the answer you had received. You stayed with it…persevering until the correct explanation has emerged."

I sat with Babaró's explanation for a moment wondering why I had been denied access to information that would have assisted me before I trusted myself to speak again. "Well, you can say that. But it took years for the correct answer to finally be revealed to me. Why so long?"

"It all has to do with aligning to the correct energy to receive."

"Oh, really," I said. My tone came off sounding like I was mocking him because I felt a bit perturbed…put off. "Seriously, Babaró, I asked the same question several times and got the same answer. What is different now? How is it that all of a sudden, now, I am aligned to receive the proper answer?"

"Simply put, it was our choice to wait until we were ready to give forth to you a little more information concerning God's gifts and the workings thereof."

"Nice, Babaró, nice." I was pretty sure Babaró could tell I was not in agreement with their decision. Not at all.

"A little more concerning that information." Babaró offered, "Tulró was the teacher who answered your question. Tulró teaches in an unusual manner that causes the student to stir—question—to expand the mind."

I smiled as I remembered some of the times Tulró had used peculiar tactics that, shall we say, were completely off the wall. Oh, yes, I understood what Babaró implied. And in my opinion Babaró was certainly correct about Tulró.

CHAPTER
FIFTEEN

There isn't a day that goes by that I do not thank God for the gifts that I am receiving! In addition, after I rise from my sleep-state the first thing I do is connect. I call to my I AM Presence (the God in me), the masters, the angels and my own spiritual guides to work through me, in me, and around me for the highest good. I open myself up to receiving God's goodness that comes in so many fantastic ways. Literally the energy flows to me and through me.

I am reminded of what my Pleiadian mother, Sarah, has taught me: Affirm with the Mighty Presence of the I AM (the God in me) that this day, as all days, are special. So I have taken that tidbit of advice and applied it to my daily life because it is God's expression through me that is creating perfection!

Something must have caught my attention because I had stopped writing to gaze out the window. As I watched the trees sway in the breeze, the awareness overcame me that there might be some really difficult times ahead of me. My father's diabetes hadn't stabilized yet. He was having mood swings with bouts of crying, night terrors, and disorientation. He just wasn't able to understand why he was in *that place and why I was stealing his money!* (Often patients with dementia and Alzheimer's will blame others for taking their personal belongings.) I was feeling awful and even guilty as if I had done this horrible thing to him. *I wonder if he will ever trust me, again?*

As the tears welled up and began to fall down my cheeks, I heard Babaró tenderly say, "I'd like to speak to you on this subject if I may." Unable to answer, I just nodded my head, yes.

"Nakala, dearest, your father is afraid. He doesn't understand what is happening to him. He is confused as the memories elude him. He wonders who can he trust? Remember Nakala, he fought in WWII. He has memories deeply embedded of continuously being in danger for literally every moment for weeks at a time. There was no relief for him. He saw his friends perish in ways that will never be repeated by those who took witness. There were times many that he thought he would perish as well. He feels that he cannot trust anyone. From one moment to the next it feels to him that he is in the wrong place! The faces are all unfamiliar. He doesn't recognize anyone. He doesn't remember why he is in the nursing home. He doesn't remember why *they* keep coming to poke him and take his blood. They keep giving him *those* shots and he doesn't understand why. It hurts. Then *they* want him to take pills. He has never been one to take even an aspirin. He'll do much better when the blood sugar has stabilized."

"Still Babaró I don't want to leave him there. Why does it have to be this way?"

"There are several reasons for this placement. For one: he is paying back karma. Two: he is unconsciously leaving his physical body more and more until the release of the soul is complete. Three: he is assisting the people who are involved in some way or another in the facility—nurses, staff, patients, and even visitors—to expand their conscious awareness and to amplify love by practicing diligence in the areas like patience, compassion, and communication. To work with these patients takes a great deal of strength in many areas. We applaud those who work with those who require care.

"May I suggest one more thing before we stop for the day?"

"Of course."

"Please send up your calls to those who are watching over those like your father. You are to direct the Legions of Light by making your request that you greatly desire their assistance with your father and those like him."

"Yes, Babaró, my heart is with my father and I will send up my prayers and requests every day."

CHAPTER
SIXTEEN

As I sat in my chair one morning, I looked at the carpet and saw it shimmering—the fibers were dancing—the Light substance that it was made from was vibrating. I sat mesmerized at the sight, thinking how weird my life had gotten.

My communications with the masters and guides seemed to be going well although I was still tired most of the time. My mind whirled from the new information that I was receiving and it was difficult to shut it down for sleep.

Religiously, every night before I slept, I had begun to practice affirmations to help me sleep, and I had seen an improvement. There still were nights, though, when I woke up to the sound of someone talking to me. I had begun to just tell them that I couldn't talk then. "If you want to talk," I would boldly state, "come by tomorrow when I am awake." Sometimes what they said caught my attention and I wanted to listen, but I knew I had to put a stop to the night visits. When they saw I was really serious, they stopped interrupting my sleep.

Finally, I felt that my life was on track. I knew what I had to do. I had dated Sam a few times, and we had enough in common that we had begun to spend a great deal of time together. In addition, Babaró had been correct about doing spiritual readings for Sam. Outwardly, everything seemed fine. I liked him okay, but energetically I felt something off that I just couldn't pinpoint.

I did sense his male energy and it was over-powering. For someone who had not had a *real* partner for…well, a long time, it was difficult for me to be around him. There had been a few times that he had massaged my feet or my neck. God it felt good to be touched…yet…I just don't know. There was just something wrong.

"Nakala?"

I heard my name and wondered if it was Nathanal who had spoken. So I asked, "Nathanal, is that you?"

"Yes," Nathanal answered, "relax for a moment. I wish to speak to you about Sam. Remember his confession concerning his addiction? He told you straight away that he likes women and a lot of them. Nakala, you disregarded his statement, his honesty. The energy that you feel is his imbalance."

"Nathanal, what I feel is so powerful and draws me in to a point that it is easy for me to feel, but I am unable to think clearly."

"It is his male prowess, his predatory expertise. He is on the hunt, Nakala. Be aware of this facet of his personality. Give your attention to his attentiveness: how he presents himself."

"What a minute…Nathanal. Babaró suggested that I work with Sam. He knew of the potential here that Sam would ask me out and then, ah, then…" my voice trailed off because I didn't want to say what I had been thinking. Then I blurted out, "I feel like I have been set up."

"Nakala you have free will *and* you have lessons to learn. Sam is not dangerous but he is considered to be a predator. Think on it. Perhaps you will understand before long."

Acknowledging that I valued his opinion, I quickly nodded my head and sighed. I wanted someone to go out with, someone who would give me his attention. Sam did that.

"Nakala, dearest, you got exactly what you asked for. You literally drew that man to you. Sam is not marriage material nor is he true to one woman. Think on this. Is this the type of man you want to keep company with?"

I noticed that Nathanal had never told me what to do or what he wanted me to do. He was asking me to look at it and figure it out for myself. Umm. Well, Sam had not given me a good reason to stop seeing him… not yet anyway.

CHAPTER
SEVENTEEN

Things between Sam and me had been going really well. We had been spending the weekends together, going to concerts and different spiritual events. I had begun hinting that maybe we should consider making our relationship more serious.

After my comments on being more committed to one another (not dating anyone else) I saw an immediate shift. He retreated somewhat and hadn't called me. I didn't think on it much.

However, it was merely two weeks later when I was talking on the phone with Sam when, out of the blue, he began telling me that he was stuck in a small motel right off of Highway 70 in western Kansas because of a snow storm. He explained that he had been asked by an *old friend* to accompany her on a trip to Colorado for a funeral. Immediately, suspicion kicked in. The way he had said, 'old friend' alerted something deep inside of me that I had better get to the bottom of this. I suspected that something was amiss. I acted like I really didn't care and waited for his full disclosure, making no comment.

The first thing was, he hadn't called me to let me know he was heading out of town. Sure funerals were sudden, so I let it go.

Sam didn't drop the subject but instead kept talking about it. I heard in his voice something different. I couldn't figure out was why he was talking to me like he was. It was as if Sam were bored or perhaps…guilty? Something strange had surfaced.

Again, Sam explained to me that *they* had been snowed in for two days in a small motel near the Colorado border. Yes, it had snowed and yes, the highway had been closed. *Was he trying to convince me?*

Right away I noticed that he was giving me way more information than I needed or wanted.

Without warning, Nathanal began to telepathically talk to me about Sam's *actual activities*. (It isn't new that a guide will talk to me telepathically while I am in a conversation with someone else. However, it was a little difficult for me to concentrate on what Nathanal was saying as he often speaks over the other person.)

Nathanal was saying that Sam had been *with her and had engaged in sexual activities*. I wasn't sure that I believed Nathanal, but I asked myself why would he (Nathanal) tell me this stuff about Sam? Then Nathanal told me outright to ask Sam if he had done the deed (gone to bed) with this woman. The pressure was so great from Nathanal that I pointedly revealed that Nathanal had been talking to me about the two of them. I paraphrased what Nathanal had said, "Nathanal has told me that you went to bed with this woman. Is this true?"

Sam knew all about Nathanal…that he was my twin flame and one of Nathanal's duties was to protect me. Of course Nathanal knew Sam's habits and what Sam had been up to.

All of the sudden I saw that Nathanal was indeed protecting me by telling me what Sam's true intentions were. Nathanal wasn't for one moment going to sit for the way I was being misled.

With Sam's response to my inquiry, I detected an edge to his voice. He was a bit on the defensive side; but he also actually whined, like a little child would when he got caught doing something bad, as he asked, "Why does it always come down to sex?" The question was rhetorical I am sure; and as I sat with it for just a moment, I wondered how utterly stupid Sam thought I was. Sam had put on a bold act all right but had totally nixed the execution of it. I had values, for crying out loud. Sam had known of my connection with Nathanal and the masters.

Evidently Sam had wanted to test the waters, so to speak, to see what he could get by with. I merely chuckled. He certainly hadn't fooled Nathanal for one second. I asked a second time, and this time he quickly admitted what he had done.

I had been warned all right. There was no need to tell me twice. Sam was not looking to be in a relationship with any *one woman*.

Politely, I told Sam, "I am through with you," and hung up the phone; never intending to speak to him again. However, Sam had other ideas. He continued to call me, working to entice me to talk about my spiritual beliefs on sexual relationships with multiple partners. No matter what I said, he continued to try to dig deeper and sway my belief on the matter so we would continue our so-called relationship while he had his varied flings.

During the first few attempts to get me to talk to him on the phone, I saw his tactic: he had been shrewd by presenting different topics on spirituality then shifted them to his beliefs on sexuality, energy, and so on. He wanted to make sure that I saw his side of the story to why he chose to have relationships with many women.

He had spoken on the subject like he had rehearsed it a thousand times before (probably to other women). He just kept saying things like the feelings are so wonderful and if we weren't meant to experience them (the physical pleasures), God wouldn't have created us this way. He went on to say, people have physical bodies and because of this we are supposed to have the physical experiences and enjoy them! Sam then said and I quote, "I view women as pieces of candy. I put several on the mantle and just look at them until I decide which flavor I desire."

I kept feeling that he might be trying to convince, not only me about his views, but himself as well. To me it seemed that he had twisted God's gift somehow to make himself feel important.

I never thought I was angry with him, just entirely flabbergasted that anyone had the nerve to play the field like he had. Finally, I told Sam that my choice was not to be with *anyone* who had several sexual partners at one time and to quit calling me. He agreed, but artfully asked if we could remain friends. I felt one thing but decided to say something else. I was simply not brave enough to say what I had been thinking which was, "Hell no, we can't be friends!" Instead I answered, "Yes, we can remain friends, but I will not go out with you again."

"Nakala," Babaró interrupted my thoughts, "won't you look at this situation a little closer?"

"Are you kidding me? Babaró, I have absolutely no desire to even talk about this to you or anyone any longer. So to 'look at it a little closer' seems a little out of the question." There was an edge to my voice, even a severity that had been unintended. Writing about Sam had stirred the pot—my pot—the pot that was full of anger.

Babaró took no offense just merely continued by channeling a long deep breath through me before he decided to speak again. "Nakala, look at this situation. I say this will teach you much about the human ego and ultimately will serve you in the future."

"Okay, Babaró, what is it that you want me to see with this situation?"

"Your comment on twisting God's gift somehow so he felt important. This is what I wish for you to examine."

"Well," I paused, not sure how to proceed with this. "He, Sam, for some reason, felt that he should be gifted with sexual pleasures from many women or be the gift…I don't know which. Maybe both? I don't know why he would think that he should have such a thing unless it was his ego making him think that the more women that go with him the better he is…at what? His prowess? Being attractive? Being a great lover? Heck I don't know what he is getting out of the relationships. I am not sure I even care."

Suddenly, the knowledge that I had reacted came full front. My anger had really flared…my very *own ego* had! "Okay, Babaró you got me. I reacted there. I am sure there is a reason for his behavior. The thing is, I was warned and I still fell for it. Then Nathanal had to come out and tell me what Sam did in order for me to really get it! I can't believe that I did that. I guess I am upset with myself for not listening to my guidance, for not taking to heart all the warning signs…*I am upset that he thought I wasn't all he needed or wanted.*"

The single word, "Correct," was the only thing that Babaró chose to say in response to my statement. I waited for several minutes to see what else might surface. But when Babaró continued to be silent, I decided to delve into the situation a little closer without his aid.

Sam had wanted reassurance that he was attractive, virile, and a self-made man. He evidently had feelings of insecurity that had been allowed to blossom into an inflated ego.

I also had feelings of insecurity. Maybe not at the same level; nevertheless, I had wanted to be appreciated by the opposite sex. I had wanted to have that special someone who would be attracted to me and who wanted *me*! Of course I had wanted a commitment with one man, not superficial liaisons. With Sam I had not succeeded because Sam required more than one woman's attention to feel good about himself. His ego had blown up so much that it required more attention or nurturing for him to continue to feel good about himself.

Even though Babaró remained quiet, he had been giving my account his full attention. Deciding that it was time he assisted, he interjected, "Nakala you require more information to put this puzzle together correctly. Sam's ego must have the food—the interactions with women—in order for it, his ego, to survive. Something you did not take entirely into consideration was the fact that you had been hinting that the two of you become a couple in your circle of friends—date exclusively. Little did you know this nudge caused a big stir on the subconscious level for Sam. The single word commitment triggered fear! What Sam did was sabotage your relationship and make sure you found out about it. This is his pattern.

"If you had gone forward with the agreement to commit to one another, Sam would not have been able to have his fill. It would have meant the death of his ego or a real rocky relationship with him. Sam was not ready for this type of transition.

"To be honest, the thought of his committing to one woman took him straight back to his marriage. He remembers, all too well, feeling trapped, unable to move freely in his pursuit of 'nourishment'. I put it like that because, quite literally, he feels as though he is starving. The need to satisfy is that immense.

"Until he realizes why he continues to run from commitment, he will continue to create the same scenarios in order to keep the ego well-fed."

"I understand Babaró," I said. But as I said those words I still recognized the sting of disappointment.

I heard my name called and knew that it had been Nathanal, and he, too, had something to contribute to the subject matter. "Nakala, I do have something I feel valuable to add to the conversation here. I desire you to know that I hold you in high esteem. I know that you do not require the 'experience' of being in that type of situation to learn about your ego. This is not a requirement for you. This is why I told you outright that Sam had strayed and not stayed true to you. Even though you suspected as much, you required him to admit his behavior to you. You were not in the place that you fully trusted your instincts but deep down you knew all right!

"I am also protector. No man will take advantage of you in this manner again!" I felt his love surge through my body and knew that Nathanal was telling me the truth. My heart expanded. I knew all right. I knew.

Sam called me a few more times, working his best to persuade me to see it his way. Each time I held my ground; I politely told him that I was not into that type of self-expression. I did not require that sort of action to feel good about who I am. Quickly I disengaged and said that I had to see to other activities.

CHAPTER
EIGHTEEN

Ironically, as soon as Sam had stopped his tactics to convert me to accept his belief concerning sexual expression, my house had sold.

Quickly, I was able to find some people who did living estates sales. The job in front of me was enormous and the people that I hired would take care of it all. All I had to do was remove or mark clearly the items I wanted to keep. They would price, sell, and do the cleanup afterwards.

I found a bungalow near my mother's residence that was perfect, so I went ahead and rented it. It was time to get on with my move.

There were so many details to see after, but so far everything was falling into alignment and I was looking forward to the change in scenery.

As I began to sort through my belongings, I found myself going through boxes of items that had belonged to my children…things they had made in art class in grade school and so on. There was one box in particular that was wooden that contained the last remnants of Bradley's life. It was so heavy that I asked my kids to come over and help me move it from the basement and go through the items. It was time to let go of treasures such as these. Along with the items were remains of several hobbies that my ex-husband had taken on and chose to leave behind. The more I took care of, the lighter I began to feel.

Most of my friends had long ago been notified of my divorce and my plans to sell my home. Many had asked where I was heading. Most were accepting of my move gracefully while others openly balked of my plans, unable to be happy that I was moving on with my life.

Momentarily hurt that anyone could judge me for being responsible by moving closer to my elderly parents, I hesitated to reassess my reasons for the change.

My own brother had bailed on me years ago when he had taken a mixture of pills. His death had not been ruled a suicide, but I felt like it had been.

As the only living child, it was up to me to take care of my parents or at least make sure they were being taken care of. I didn't feel like I would be away from Kansas City for an extended period…yet one never knows what the future has in store for us. Kansas City had been my home for the last twenty-five years.

Thoughts of returning to my home town, where I had lived until I had married, surfaced, and I felt in my heart that if I had truly been given any other sort of a choice to move to, that place wouldn't have been it. I felt as if I had grown past all of that. The town had taught me what I needed to know.

However, on the flip side of it all, I loved my parents and wanted to be near them. Taking care of family business, long distance, was taking way too much out of me. I assured myself that the move was temporary and I'd be back.

So my moving date was set for the following Thanksgiving. I made my plans known to the couple who were in charge of my living estate sale. They knew well of my situation. Quite unexpectedly they offered, "We can help you out. We have family down in Wichita and we were planning on being there that weekend anyway. We'll be happy to drive the truck for you. You take your car."

It isn't like I can see Nathanal or the other guides and masters who work with me in physical form…because they are not like someone of the physical. Their bodies vibrate so fast that we are unable to see them. They would literally have to slow down their vibration in order for us to see them. But there are times when I can *sense* certain things. This had been one of those times. Nathanal had been watching me…my facial expressions, my aura, and listening to my innermost thoughts. I saw him smiling and chuckling to himself.

"Oh, I get it Nathanal," I said telepathically, "You organized all of this." While I had been unable to fathom an arrangement like this, he had put it all together so easily. It certainly had been a win win situation. Everyone involved would benefit from the arrangement. "Thank you, Nathanal."

There are no coincidences. Nathanal had lined this up. He had found people who would benefit from my situation as well as I.

The three of us agreed on the date and time of departure. I gave them the address where we would unload. As we continued to talk about what I had been working on in Wichita, I told them I was cleaning out my father's place as well.

Suddenly another piece was being revealed. With my father's things they could make the estate sale even bigger. They would unload my furniture at my new home, drive across town, load up my father's stuff, and they would drive it all back to sell at my house. Slick!

CHAPTER
NINETEEN

There was simply too much for me to do during the moving process for me to continue to write my book. Regrettably, I set it aside and concentrated on getting settled in my new place. But that didn't stop the communications from continuing with the Beings of Light. I continued to receive guidance and daily dictations from the masters, other beings from the angelic realm, and those that I had never heard of before as well. The subjects they chose to speak on were varied, after which others then began to build upon their teachings. I created journals for some of the beings who had indicated they would be back. Daily I wrote in my personal journal, documenting different experiences, and messages that I telepathically received.

Even though I was busy, I stewed about Kazmar…whether he still wanted to work with me after I got settled. Because I had become familiar with some of the methods of the masters for teaching, I also wondered if Kazmar might be simply another persona of one of the teachers. I had a suspicion that Babaró or another master may have made up this guy, Kazmar.

Every few days, I brought up Kazmar's name in hopes that he was around and I would be able to speak with him. Each time I was always told that he was waiting for me and would wait until the alignment had been made for us to work together. But still I wasn't sure—couldn't be sure—because I didn't know what these guys had in mind concerning this particular teaching. Would he really wait around for me until I had enough time to sit and listen to his ideas or take dictation from him?

Without prior notice, my vibration rose and I knew that I had company. Someone took over my body and began to do movements with my neck to massage my muscles, but no one spoke. There was no attempt to announce who had taken over. Fastidiously, I made it a point not to ask. Instead, I just waited to see how long it would take before this being decided to get on with it. Surprisingly, my vibration rose even higher and I heard a man's voice say, "This is Babaró. Relax with it, will you?"

I felt my heart expand and Babaró's love pour through me. For a moment, I thought I would cry, the love felt so good. But then I felt the energy in my solar plexus shift and I became a little uncomfortable. I noticed that my hands tingled. No longer did I have the desire to write. I closed my eyes and felt love go through my body, wave after wave. My heart began to beat faster until at last the energy began to subside a bit.

I had completely relaxed when I heard Babaró say, "I stand behind you in your aura, Nakala. You feel my presence, my love. This is part of why I am here: to assist in raising your vibration. I uplift you with my radiation. This assists your body in becoming comfortable with the higher vibrations. In other words, you are adapting to the energies of the higher beings: the Masters and the Christed Ones.

"Nakala, you are to remember to breathe in deeply when you are gifted like just now. What I give is healing energy. You became uncomfortable because you are not open to receiving in full measure. For you what I give is a bit too intense, but this is to be, as I must continue to challenge you by expanding and amplifying my radiation. Do you see?" I merely nodded my head, yes, as I did not want to be distracted by speaking.

"Nakala, the man, Kazmar is in wait for you to begin your time to work together. Perhaps, I stand back for a time and see what he has to offer. Remember the writings may always be discarded."

Babaró's words prompted me to remember the time I had thrown in the trash over two hundred pages of work with the wave of his hand. Momentarily, I had questioned his directive; and then as if I hadn't spent literally months of my life writing the narrative, I had swiftly surrendered.

At last, the time had come for me to see what Kazmar was made of—what his expertise was. Suddenly, I grew uneasy—unsure of myself.

It seemed as if in the far distance I could hear someone make a sound like he were clearing his throat. Masters do not clear their throats was all I could think. They had no reason for this action.

I heard it again. I could tell there was something wrong with my connection. I said, "Maybe I am not attuned correctly. I am having trouble hearing you."

"Ah." He paused briefly then asked, "Is this better, Nakala?" At once I could hear him perfectly, but I still had no idea who it was.

My lips curved into a smile and I intuitively knew. It was Kazmar. Kazmar channeled a single nod affirming his identity.

"Yes, you have correct," Kazmar said. Immediately I noticed that his speech was a little different than the last time we had talked.

"My aim is to hold your attention while I dictate the words through you as you type. My name is indeed Kazmar!"

As if the question had been projected, I asked myself now where did he say he was from? I went into my memory to retrieve the information but found the memory elusive.

Kazmar said, "I am from Venus. How quickly you forget important details.

"Indeed, master I am at writing, yes. I have no need to clear my throat as you say. It is, however, a subtle way to attract your attention. There are times I do not wish to interrupt your thoughts or what you are giving yourself over to. (The activity you are involved in.)"

I couldn't contain myself any longer. I wanted to know so I asked the ten million dollar question, "Are you an ascended master?"

"No," he replied, "I am flirting with adventure. Breathe easy Nakala. You are in no danger." Quickly, I detected that he had taken the words directly from my vision board that hung behind my desk.

I heard what Kazmar said, yet I still felt uneasy with this arrangement. His way of speaking was different than I was accustomed to, and I still had this uncanny feeling.

Kazmar was trying to relieve my tension when he stated, "There is absolutely no reason for you to become distressed with our bargain. I will give hence some of my best prose and you may decide for yourself what you wish of me. Perhaps you say, 'Be gone!' Or perhaps you fall in love with me and beg me, 'Kazmar stay on forever!' I say, my aim is to please you no matter what you decide!"

I felt my vibration rise and knew that this fellow, whoever he is, was a romantic and using his words to charm, seduce me to win my favor. Thinking I knew his angle, I unintentionally chuckled. *This ought to be real good.*

I was guided to look at the time and saw that it showed five o'clock. Unfortunately my writing time had come to an end for the day and I would not be able to type Kazmar's "prose".

✳ ✳ ✳

I had awoken earlier than usual and popped straight out of bed without delay. The writing called me; Kazmar called me. Unfortunately, different responsibilities took priority, detaining me from my work. All the while my arrangement with Kazmar stayed in the forefront of my mind. I was looking forward to hearing Kazmar talk. I wanted to know more about this fellow. I had found he had a distinct style of speaking for sure, but what would he choose to write about? Would he choose to present me words like beautiful bouquets of flowers with the fragrance so sweet that my sensibilities were lifted?

I decided to light a candle before I sat down to write, acknowledging and honoring my teams from Pleiades, who are members of Telbar and the Comterous, the angels and masters, and other guides who come from the higher realms to offer their wisdom or healing radiation. I offered my call, "To the Highest Most Divine Awareness, work through me, in me, and around me for the highest good. May these writings serve to assist the people of our world by teaching them that we are indeed not alone and are well cared for!"

At once my attention was directed to my vision board. I saw, 'Born to' then my eyes shifted to another area of the vision board and I read 'Travel' and thought that perhaps the person (Light Being) was easing into the subject matter of the day.

I heard, "Yes, you are correct." But still I hadn't been told who would be teaching through me for this portion of the book.

I heard the words, "It is I, Kazmar." But I was left confused because his tone of voice had changed so dramatically. Who was this fellow who was so eager to please? In his voice I had recognized the nuances of someone from Far East India—one who had achieved high status—culture and discipline—and great wealth.

Immediately, in my mind's eye, I saw the crowded street markets of one of the larger cities of India. It was as if I had been transported there and stood looking on at the traffic of all the people perusing the wares of the day. I had a clear view of both sides of the dirt street. The vendors had stacks of baskets, tables loaded with bobbles and trinkets. Some vendors had hung yards of brightly colored silk and cotton fabrics for sale. The marketing I felt clever because the fabrics also served as an invitation for shoppers to come closer…to step out of the hot sun if only for a moment.

In fascination, I watched the fabrics flutter in the breeze. There beside the merchants with all the beautiful fabrics was another vendor selling an assortment of leavened and flat breads. The aroma overtook. It was as if I had been actually transported there walking among the shoppers, experiencing it all as they were. To my left I noticed several tables with different fruits and vegetables (many I didn't recognize) heaped to overflowing.

Suddenly, the dirt from the street took flight and the people quickly covered their faces. I looked up into the sky and saw the darkness beginning to overtake. A storm was brewing. The vendors began to move items closer to the walls of the buildings while others began to box up their wares to leave. They moved with precision as if they had done this same thing many times in the past.

As I observed the scene of the India market, I determined that it all had been projected into my mind.

India…umm. It hadn't been so long ago that Nathanal had asked me to go to India. I had thought about it for about two seconds then had given him a solid answer, one that indicated I would not be swayed.

A breath was suddenly channeled through me assisting me to relax a bit. The time Nathanal had talked of India had bothered me. Emotions had risen of distaste. I had told him that I had no desire to visit that place. The reputation of the heat and dirt had been more than enough to deter me. But secretly, I had wondered if perhaps there might be a different reason why I didn't want to go there. It could have been a past life. From the way I felt, I suspected my stay hadn't been so pleasant.

I stopped writing for a moment and heard a man with the Indian accent telepathically say, "Yes, I would like you to visit India. My country is beautiful. I would like to share the sights with you."

Quite honestly, I wondered how *we* had gotten on the topic of India. I had not changed my mind. The place did not appeal to me. I did not answer Kazmar directly, but I knew that he had either heard me, saw what I had written, or felt my aversion concerning the topic.

"Nakala, you do not know who I am, what my intentions are. I desire greatly to teach you to be open to possibilities that are presented to you!"

"Yes," I nodded my head, "I understand. But for some reason the country of India doesn't appeal to me. I would much rather visit Europe, Spain, to be exact. From there I have not decided."

"Know this, Nakala. There will be a time in the very near future when you travel to India. It is time that you go, if only for a brief visit."

I didn't respond, just thought to myself, "Here we go again."

"Now, I offer this to you. You are a traveler. We all are. Yes, there are those who remain in one town during particular embodiments, but when they pass from the physical form they travel. This is what happens. You are meant to experience all."

I felt myself digging in, like I was being dragged behind a runaway horse and was trying with all my might to stop it! There was a certain feeling of dread concerning what Kazmar was proposing. But I kept my cool and replied in a detached manner, "Well, I can certainly understand and appreciate *your* opinion. But this *trip* to India…you know I am real sure I have been there before and once was plenty enough."

"Nakala, let me take you back…." I stopped listening, knowing what he wanted to do. Adamantly, I protested shaking my head, no. I did not want to have a past life regression. They often were traumatic, and I just didn't want to deal with another unfortunate death that had resulted from a set of unjust reasons!

I sensed that Kazmar wasn't going to give up so easy. There was some sort of reason he was bringing up the subject, and I knew he wouldn't just forget this conversation. As I saw it, he could either keep talking as I pretended to listen, openly object to my decision, or perhaps he might bring it up another time when I had softened a bit.

The last time one of the masters had done a life regression with me, I saw myself held in stocks, probably in England in the 1600's. I had been held there immobile for three unbearable days as punishment for making herbal remedies.

At least once during my stay, my husband and two children walked past me on a path going on an errand. They, none of them, had glanced my way, unable to for fear of the backlash of the town officials. I knew there had been nothing they could do. I had always felt that I had been killed afterward: beheaded or hung or perhaps burned at the stake…maybe that had been another embodiment though.

That regression had been similar to reliving it. Well…not nearly as bad. But I felt the humility of it all…the shame. That had been one of the easier regressions. But it had stuck with me, nonetheless. I kept seeing myself placed on a wooden platform built a few feet higher than the ground level for the "spectators" to have an easier look. I had worn a roughly woven (probably linen) grey dress. The skirt had been full. I was bent over, unable to sit, with my head and hands stuffed through the roughly hewn holes made in the heavy wooden planks. I had felt the rough wood wear at my skin. I saw the blood.

There had been several times when I wondered if they had been so cruel as to deny me the opportunity to go into the woods to relieve myself, have some food, or even sips of water. I suspected not. I had been placed there for the entire town to take witness of. The message that I had given to the towns-people by my torment had screamed in my mind. *Do not defy the town council or this is what will happen to you.*

There had been other regressions, enough so that I didn't care to have any more ever again.

"Breathe easy, Nakala. What I have for you is a bit more straightforward than what you have experienced in the past. India is a fascinating place. Mystics, yogis, and masters have made this place their home. To learn about the culture would be most valuable for you."

I wasn't feeling all that great about the conversation and wanted Kazmar to please drop it when he said, "You will be guided when the time is correct for you."

Even though Kazmar was willing to drop the topic of India, he was not ready to drop his willingness to converse with me.

"There is nothing more," Kazmar stated, "that I wish to add to *convince* you that India is a place that would assist you in the expansion of all that you are. It would be my pleasure to escort you to the place I call my home." My vibration rose considerably and I knew that Kazmar was sincere about his request…his offer.

"Well, Kazmar," I said, "someday, perhaps, I will take you up on your proposal; but for now I think it is best that I stay here and tend to my parents."

"Another day, then perhaps."

For now, Kazmar politely let the subject drop of visiting India.

* * *

I thought I was finished for the day. There was a build-up of energy. I figured to release it I should get up and do something physical. But there had been no indication that my time was finished. I was directed, again, to look at my vision board to the word, "Now."

After several neck rolls, Kazmar exclaimed, "We begin!"

CHAPTER
TWENTY

Even though I had clearly heard the excitement in Kazmar's declaration, we didn't begin. My phone rang. It being Crystal, I wanted to answer it. In this case, I did not even consider asking for guidance, like I normally would have, if it were my highest good to take the call at that moment. I knew that Kazmar wanted to write. But for some unknown reason I was resisting. Why?

Leisurely, as if I had nothing else to do, I talked to Crystal for a good forty-five minutes. As our conversation came to an end, I glanced at the clock and saw that it was 5:00 PM. Quitting time!

For me to work beyond 5:00 PM was a rare occasion. The master I wrote under always determined when we would finish. However, now I did not hear the words, "It is time that we lay down the writings for today."

Rather, what I heard was Kazmar stating in an exceedingly firm tone, that I get back to my desk because *he* had not finished *his* dictation. Well, okay then.

I wasn't happy with his directive. However, I realized that it had been my choice to take the phone call during dictations. I sighed and agreed to his request all the while remembering I had free will here with this choice. During the entire writing session I had felt a pressure in my solar plexus that I didn't understand. Perhaps it was Kazmar's energy or maybe I was afraid we would not be a good match somehow, and I would have to confront the issue. *What was so important that he keep me longer?*

"Nakala," Kazmar began in earnest, "It isn't my desire to be so strict with our arrangement that you are held over past your usual writing time. However, I do request that you be considerate of *My* time. I offer you my hand, my expertise! I feel that we, together, can make a go of it if you will honor me with your presence."

Oh, boy, realizing the magnitude of how inconsiderate and downright rude I had been, I stated, "I am so sorry. I have felt...I know this is no excuse but the energy—your energy, maybe—is causing me to be fidgety. I have gotten up at least eight times in the last three hours. It is like I want to run away for some reason. I realize that I might be avoiding something. Right now I feel a vibration in my entire body. It feels good yet for some reason at this time I feel unsettled."

Kazmar knew, of course, what I had been feeling. I was hoping at some point through the writing he might address the issue. But not now! Now I just wanted to go outdoors or do something else that would take me far away from the office, my computer...working to type their thoughts... my thoughts. I wanted peace.

"Nakala," Kazmar began ever so softly, "I desire to assist you here. My energy—my Light—my vibration thereof is what is causing you to feel ill at ease. Because of where I stand, your body feels and for you it is un- comfortable. You are learning to accept and integrate my Light. Breathe deeply and consciously bring in the awareness to expand and align your chakra (your heart) with my energy please. Open your heart to accept me, my gifts."

As I did as he suggested, I felt myself surrender to his Presence and there was only Love. I felt my vibration rise even more. I had no desire to continue to write.

Suddenly I heard, "It is I Telmure! I AM come!"

"What?" was all I could manage.

"I have come for you, Nakala. You are like my daughter and I shall al- ways care for you as such."

The name Telmure was familiar. "I remember your name," I said, "you are of the Akasie family. You are one of the elders?"

I saw him nod his head as he confirmed my statement, "Yes. I am in- deed. I AM come to assist you in this hour."

I thought back to Kazmar and asked, "What happened to him? Kazmar?"

"I am Kazmar."

Trying to still time, I furrowed my eyebrows, and tilted my head puzzled. "Wait! I don't understand. Why did you come and identify yourself as Kazmar?"

"Nakala, dear one, it was a teaching to expand your conscious awareness. You have taken on the belief that the masters of Comterous are in total command of the books that you write together. I say look to your Beloved I AM Presence (the God in you) and command and demand that, through you, the books are always written perfectly, pleasing to His Divine Will!

"Nakala, you are God's expression in physical form. Perfect you are in every way."

My vibration went higher and I felt his love pour through me. "I am not perfect, Telmure, not even close."

"Ah, Nakala, it is your Divine Essence, your true Holy Christ Self that IS perfect. It is the ego, the expression of the human self and personality that is not perfect. Look to the God quality in you only!"

"Telmure, I work at that every day and, to be honest, some days I feel I am a total train wreck. My thoughts take over that are created straight from my ego and it goes downhill from there."

Telmure chose not to address my last statement but rather chose to talk about the character, Kazmar. I took note that I had this subtle knowing all along that something hadn't been quite right concerning this guy.

"What I did was invent another personality, Kazmar, to present to you an opportunity to examine your role as a writer. You currently hire out certain jobs like the editing and so on to get the books complete to market. You are to use discernment in many situations concerning the production of the books.

"As you learn to connect with your I AM Presence, you will understand that this is how you choose those who come to you for work."

As Telmure spoke I remembered that several years back I had been presented an idea about beginning my own publishing company. I had thought long and hard on it and even purchased the domain name on the Internet to ready myself for the possibility. To date, however, nothing had occurred. I knew in my heart what I wanted. It was a matter of manifesting my desires. The timing I left to God.

"So…Telmure, this Kazmar fellow doesn't actually exist? You literally created the character in order to expand my belief that I have more say in the writing process than I originally thought?"

"Nakala, it is your Beloved I AM Presence that has the say, the Power. Connect and receive the guidance that is God's Perfection."

A few moments passed. I felt that Telmure's last statement brought his teaching to a close. Perhaps he would excuse me for the rest of the day.

Then I heard Telmure say, "I am a guardian at best."

I hadn't understood his meaning and hesitated. I simply didn't want to type the words before I felt the reader would have clarity.

I reviewed his words 'I am a guardian at best'. From what I knew about Telmure, all signs pointed in the direction that he was high on the ladder of the hierarchy of the Akasie. He, Telmure, probably was near the top. So why the words, "I am guardian at best?" I sat for several minutes waiting for him to elaborate on his statement. Nothing happened. Nothing was said. I shrugged my shoulders and remembered what I had done earlier to him by answering the phone call from Crystal in lieu of fulfilling my promise to write. I put my elbows on the table and rested my chin in my hands and looked at the vision board and saw 'Game On!' I literally groaned out loud and said to myself, "Oh, would these guys ever tire of using the vision board as a way of communicating with me?"

"See here, Nakala. How is it that you communicate with your peers who share the physical world with you?"

Oh, I must have hit a sore spot here. Telmure's tone indicated that he was about to fill me in on something that he considered to be of vital importance.

"You write letters, e-mails, texts, and make calls on the phone. There is radio, TV, and video. Technology has advanced so much that there are several gadgets like MP3 players and other devices to carry forth images and sound in order to communicate.

"When you are in the company of someone you communicate with, you are constantly observing body language whether you realize it or not: facial expression and the body posture. You may hold hands or touch the person's body in some way. As a way to communicate, you may open a door, serve a refreshment, or an entire meal. You may join for a meeting of some sort to enhance your community or the World. You may have a celebration. You may call the attention of someone with your voice.

"On a fourth dimensional or energetic level you can telepathically send a communication with your thoughts and emotions.

"Teachers speak, use hand gestures, their bodies, write on caulk boards, dry erase boards, and send assignments and such on computers and other devices to communicate with their students. Artists may use several different media to communicate with people. Musicians communicate through their music. Communication methods are endless…the way we express is unlimited! One more thing: when someone walks away from a conversation or statement this is also a communication."

Audibly I heard myself sigh and said, "Yes, Telmure, I understand that walking away from our session earlier was a communication that said my phone call was more important than my agreement. I didn't respect you at all. Again, I apologize."

"Nakala, what you did was send a message to me, indeed a very clear message that you didn't care enough about your agreement to uphold it."

"Look Telmure, I feel that we have discussed this to the ground. I said I am sorry. I will not *ever* do that again."

"Nakala, if you desire time off. Just ask. Your team takes your commands. You are to assess your requirements in order to stay balanced. Look at the Divine Matrix of which you are and know what you need. You have agreed to this contract to write many books with the Comterous. This is what makes your heart sing. However, if you are out of sorts and require an adjustment of some sort, please make it. We desire the books to be filled with Light! This means that you write only when *you* are filled with Light!"

PART

SIX

PAST LIVES

CHAPTER
TWENTY-ONE

Through my daily meditations, there were times that I was able to connect with some of my family members who had already passed over like my brother and my son. Always, I found some measure of healing from the experience.

On many occasions, I would record in my journal the dialogue between myself and these people in hopes that if I could review the conversation again that would help me understand on a deeper level why they both had decided to leave this world so early in their lives: before they had reached their full potential or fulfilled certain responsibilities. Because I love life so much and love living here, checking out like they both had done seemed inconceivable to me.

The times I had talked to Bradley I had spoken to him as his mother would, working to validate his feelings. In turn, I had spoken of what I thought about his decision…that frankly I hadn't understood what had happened. Throughout our conversations I had encouraged him to speak openly about his feelings. But as I remember, he really hadn't; he listened to me talk about all of us making mistakes. We were all sorry.

Our sessions hadn't happened one after another. Many weeks had passed in between. Now, as I think on it, perhaps the meetings had been staged apart in order that we process each conversation before we talked again. Emotions had been palpable with healing occurring on a tangible level.

Even though Bradley never really explained why he had decided to commit suicide, (maybe he had never really understood his action himself), I had been able to let go of another layer of hurt.

I believe it was during the last session with Bradley when he had agreed to work with the angelic teachers. The tears had flowed freely and the feelings of love were strong. I really missed my son and still do but knew that he had to go with the Beings of Light in order to heal and move on.

"Nakala please listen to me." I felt Quem's strength and love all rolled up in one neat package. I closed my eyes and focused on the love I felt, not wanting to listen to his words. Soon the energy subsided a bit, allowing me to shift my awareness and listen to his teaching. "People build momentums around certain beliefs that manifest in certain actions. Concerning Bradley, when you had your conversations with him he had not had the understanding of what had driven him to his impulsive behavior. He didn't understand that he even had acted impulsively! He had built a very strong impetus around ending his life when things got scary or he just didn't like what was happening. He had obsessed about a way to end his struggle for two years. Simply put he merely wanted a way out."

I was shocked at what Quem said because I didn't recall Bradley being defiant, argumentative, or causing problems that far back. "What? He had wanted to die that far back? Seriously?"

"Look to the dates, Nakala."

"What do you mean 'look to the dates'?"

"In the beginning, for Bradley, it was just a fleeting thought. Kurt Cobain's suicide offered much food for thought and after a while the thoughts came more frequently until they consumed him. (Kurt had been a popular Seattle grunge musician who openly expressed his depression and the like through public interviews and his lyrics. He had died April 5, 1994.) This was just one part of why Bradley made certain choices."

I saw that Kurt had killed himself a little over a year before Bradley had done the same thing. *What had happened before that to make him what to escape?*

"You saw that he had exhibited behaviors that were reckless...life threatening, in fact, long before Kurt's death...as far back as 1984, the year your younger son was born. However, your explanation had been that Bradley's behaviors were curious, getting him into precarious situations that, yes, could have easily ended his life.

"Life seemed no longer important to him. This is how he had operated in past lives, as well. He simply had made it his way. This was a very focused ambition, if you will, that he had created and nurtured—thought, feeling, and yes, action—building more intensity over the ages."

Unmistakably, I could see that Quem wanted me to understand more of why Bradley had chosen that particular path (to commit suicide) instead of what most people do and that is to face up to any given situation or problem and work through it. Instead, Bradley had been creating more mental challenges and had infused those thoughts with an exceptional amount of fuel (feeling). Maybe to *check out* had been his solution. He wouldn't have to pay penance for all the trouble he had created. As illogical as it sounds, he seriously may have thought he could take care of it all in one clean strike. It seemed to me that Bradley just didn't care or perhaps had a defeatist attitude. At any rate, for me, to identify with Brad's choices had been impossible because I had never felt so depressed that I wanted to end my life.

On this level of perception, the only thing I could figure out was that Bradley had been really unhappy. In hindsight, I knew as a parent that I had made choices that weren't for his highest good, although I knew, for my level of awareness, I had done everything in my power to care for him and protect him so he knew that I loved him. Guilt should not have been one of the emotions I had felt after his passing. On the contrary, guilt had played a huge role, immobilizing my progress toward healing.

I had looked at other families who had lived through volatile situations like ours or even far worse. Their children were able to cope and some even had excelled in the face of their extreme adversity.

We loved our children and as a family had been, for the most part, stable, responsible, resourceful, and honest. We were respected in our community. Scott had encouraged the boys to be involved in Boy Scouts. Although Bradley had decided he didn't want to continue with the meetings, he had continued to go camping and canoeing with the boys and our family. He had never been forced to follow through with the group but had always been encouraged.

The kids had animals that they took care of. Bradley had a dog and took care of him. We took them on outings, had meals together; and I had motivated them to express themselves by decorating their rooms and picking out their clothes. I did not dictate how they would have their hair. We were not wealthy by any means, but we had a steady income and were able to provide for our family. I made sure they attended school and had time with their friends. So what had gone wrong? I couldn't answer my question because there had not been anything that I could see that would have caused this type of despondent outlook and action.

Again, I studied all of the signs and nothing really jibed. The only area I felt we had neglected had been teaching them that we are spiritual beings. But then, how could we teach something we didn't know about. Sure we knew there was a God, but that was it. We didn't have any background on Spirit.

The more I wrote, the worse I began to feel. I shook my head in defiance and wondered what the point to all of this was.

Quem spoke up then saying, "Nakala, when Bradley first passed, you agonized over these types of details: the 'if only I had done this,' and, the whys. You are doing it again. Over and over you are taking apart piece by piece what you could have done differently and what the real triggers were for him to hang himself.

"Through the different times I worked with you on this issue, I explained that Bradley had made it a habit to *check out*, as you call it. Bradley's practice had been to quit when things got a little tough. However, I had never given you any details.

"Before we get into the past lives, I wish to show you something," Quem began. "Some teenagers have taken to watching many hours of TV every day and playing violent video games (often unmonitored). These are fairly new past times for your children, but have already established themselves deeply in your culture. Music is a big influence as well. Bradley was entertained by these activities, but also with these activities he had been in the process of being programed.

"In addition, Bradley had been mimicking his idol, Kurt Cobain. Bradley thought so much of the musician that he named his dog after him."

"Oh, yes."

"These are all activities and events that influenced your son. Bradley had a young, impressionable mind and had exhibited impulsive decision-making, and at times these choices had been life threatening. Because of past life momentums—suicide—he had been easily *inspired,* shall we say, to take his own life when he perceived things as difficult.

"Bradley was so very vulnerable. Nakala, you have forgotten the teaching on negative entities, have you not?"

"Oh, God! Yes, I did forget. He had entities? Where on earth did he get them?"

"Dear one, not just yet do I wish to address your question.

"Nakala, you didn't know this but he had had a crush on a girl. Being sexually frustrated was another issue at play. It is time to get on with it. I wish you to understand that what Bradley did was not your fault. Please release yourself from the burdens of guilt and responsibility."

"Oh, Quem, I know that I have come a long way with my feelings, but I am still responsible. I should have been able to keep my son safe."

"Nakala, do you not recall you had quit your job a year before to stay at home and to watch over your children closer? Even so, you cannot watch anyone twenty-four hours a day, seven days a week. It is impossible. You require rest and your own life. Remember that Bradley was the one to make that choice."

Quem had stopped his transmission. Momentarily, I shut my eyes and rested for a moment. I felt the heaviness of my mind and decided that I could use a nap.

"Quem, I could use a few minutes to myself. Do you mind?"

"Of course not, my young daughter, go. I will be here when you get back."

When I got to my room I hit the pillow hard and pulled the covers up intending to sleep for thirty minutes or so but, instead, I heard a voice softly speaking to me lulling me into a subdued state of consciousness.

I was taken into a small, dark, damp log cabin. The fireplace was burning, taking the chill out of the air just a bit. But I noticed that soon it would burn down if someone didn't tend to it soon. I wanted to move closer to it but for some reason stood still and watched from another vantage point.

It was as if I had been transported into another time and space. I merged my consciousness with a young woman probably in her early twenties… yet it felt as if I were looking at the scene from another perspective, another dimension; and the woman was still a separate being.

There was a single window in the entire place that allowed a tiny bit of light into the room. However, it was so gloomy outdoors that I couldn't tell if it was early morning, evening, or just cloudy. Everything was so dark! I didn't see any lamps or candles lit. The room was sparsely furnished except for a few basic pieces: a roughly hewn table and two benches. Over by the stone fireplace there were two chairs. One was a rocking chair with a quilt lying in its seat. I saw a doorway off of the area that had to be a kitchen even though there was little there that indicated there was any baking or cooking going on. I figured the room off to the side must be a bedroom but all I saw was darkness. There were some pots and utensils hanging on wooden pegs that hung over some wooden planks that were attached to the kitchen wall. I saw a butter churn, a coffee grinder, and a basket of old apples sitting near the corner.

I saw the woman, whom I somehow knew to be myself, walk to the front door and open it and step out. I looked down at the dirt and saw the outline of my light gray cotton dress: my stomach bulged. I was very pregnant. Protectively, I put my hands on it.

There was a little overhang of roof that kept a small patch of earth relatively dry in front of the door. Nothing else looked dry. The rain looked like it had been coming down in a steady stream for days with no intention of letting up any time soon. I saw large puddles here and there and made a mental note of the open area directly in front of the cabin. I perused the topography assessing the features. *For what?*

I looked beyond the open area, seeing a gradual downward slope in the landscape that had collected a sufficient amount of water like a small pond was being birthed. Everything was wet and muddy. Looking up into the dark sky, I prayed. I heard myself whisper, "God save my baby. Save me." *From what?*

Suddenly, I felt really strange and recognized that I was utterly afraid and wanted to run as fast and as far away as I could from this place. Again, I looked down at my stomach.

Glancing up, I gauged the distance from the front of the house to the far end of the cleared area to the thicket of trees. I saw the large areas of water and mud, knowing if I stepped in it I would sink down to my knees. I bowed my head, knowing that it was positively hopeless. There were trees everywhere. I couldn't see a road or even a path. The feelings of desperation overtook me. I had to get out of here was all I could think. *But why?*

There were tree stumps in the open area reminding me of the previous season of crops and how little we had managed to harvest.

Burr, I pulled my shawl closer around me and began to turn to step back into the house when I saw the man who I instinctively knew was my husband, Jacob.

In a mere moment I took in the sight of him. His long dark stringy hair hung loose around his greasy, sweaty face. He hadn't shaved or bathed in some time. The odor of his body filled my nostrils and I thought I would gag. He looked thin, malnourished, with dark circles under his eyes like he hadn't slept for days. His clothes were homespun and were much too large for his thin frame. Tattered leather suspenders held up his pants. His boots were worn to the point that I thought they probably had holes in the soles.

Turning to look outdoors and assess the situation once more, I was startled by a loud bang. I had been holding on to the doorframe and felt the roughness of wood as I turned to see Jacob with his fist on the thick planks of wood that made the table as if it were glued there. His body literally trembled with rage as he glared at me. Daring, I looked up into his eyes and met his stare, one on one, and saw they were glazed over; his pupils were dilated as if he had gone completely mad! Fear surged through me and I knew that my life depended on clear thinking: I had to save myself. My baby depended on me!

Drips of sweat ran down Jacob's face and neck; the underarms and chest area of his shirt were dirty and damp. Suddenly the memory flashed of an argument we had been having. He had been screaming at me. *About what?* I had opened the door intending to flee and saw how futile my thoughts were.

Gripping the doorframe for support I felt my knees buckle. In slow motion I saw Jacob turn for his shotgun that had rested in a niche by the fireplace. He took it, aiming it straight at me. I gasped. In a single instant it was finished. I screamed, turned to run, but not fast enough. The shot blasted through the air. All I heard was muffled silence as I fell to the ground into oblivion.

✳ ✳ ✳

I gasped! "Oh, my God! Quem," I asked, "What am I seeing?"

Quem didn't respond to my question. Instead, I was taken back to the scene before me. As if watching from above I saw myself in the threshold lying halfway outdoors on the dirt porch as the ground hungrily drank in my blood.

Jacob stood there for what it seemed to be an eternity. Then he moved closer to my crumpled body and looked down into my ashen face. He didn't yell, cry, touch me, or even attempt to move me. Instead, in a stupor, he quietly shuffled past me, unhurriedly reached for a rope that had been hanging from the wall, and walked toward the woods. It was as if he no longer were able to think or feel! Everything had shut down.

Being overcome by emotion, I temporarily had gone off somewhere, my mind blank void of thought and feeling. Quem gently brought me back and said, "Nakala, dear one, what you saw was a previous life with your departed son who then played the role of your husband."

I heard the sound of someone whimpering and realized it was I. The images had been so real. The sounds I heard…the rain…the gun shot. My fear had been intense, over-riding my own present reality. I had known that it would come to this sooner or later. I had wanted to flee but in my condition I knew that I wouldn't get far.

I swallowed hard and wiped the tears from my face, beginning to understand what Quem had been explaining about past momentums.

"Quem, he shot me. Oh, my God. I lay there and died, didn't I?"

Instead of answering me in a straightforward manner, Quem decided to give me more detail. "This life-stream or experience was in the 1800's in America. I have selected very few lives to share with you for one purpose. You are not ready to see all.

"This life-stream I preferred to expound on will reveal much. You were husband and wife. Yes, his name, Jacob and yours was Agatha. You were seven months pregnant. Jacob was severely depressed. You lived on acreage (a fair amount) that he farmed. He had been clearing that acreage of trees and rocks. However, he hadn't been able to get outdoors much as the rains were heavy for an extended period of weeks. The sun's rays were hidden most of the time. In addition, he hadn't been able to get the crops planted.

"There were several forces at play here that contributed to his depression: the lack of sunshine, inability to get outdoors, and the failure to get crops in the ground. He was powerless, as nature would not be leashed.

"We are talking about the nourishment of the human body by the way of sunshine, nature, and food. But that wasn't the entirety of it. His family (you and the unborn babe) depended on him for food and there was nothing he could do. To him the situation seemed impossible. He saw what he faced, Nakala. His choices were limited on how to proceed. This was to be your first child; your marriage had been fairly young. The cupboards were nearly bare. He saw no solution, no way to feed you. He had been unable to sleep. He had been rife with guilt, anger…hate! His temper flared, Nakala, often, and so did yours. You faced immense pressure.

"Nakala, he took the shot gun to you after one of your arguments. None of your vital organs were hit, but the baby was lost. With the loss of blood you had been in danger of dying as well. He saw the blood, what he had done. Thinking you were dead he had gone out into the woods, ending it there.

"All along a sister of yours, Suzanne, had planned to visit in a day or two. This too had been a source of tension, the impetuous excuse of your argument. He saw himself as a failure. Your sister arrived a little earlier than planned. There she found you and nursed you back to health.

"This wasn't the first time this soul (your then husband) finished things in this fashion. As I said he had made it a habit, even routine, if you will.

"Nakala, after Bradley passed from his earthly body his spirit remained in your household for several years. He had only been fourteen and had limited knowledge. He had refused the angels who had summoned him to come with them when he exited the physical body.

"During the first few years, after Bradley's passing, you became acutely aware of the electrical interferences and so on. You questioned their source. Bradley had been very angry before and after his suicide, as well.

After his rash decision, he saw, all too plainly, what he had gotten himself into. He wasn't able to communicate with any of you; but because of the results of his anger; he began to see that he could manipulate energy somewhat. At first it wasn't intentional, but after a few times he got the gist of it. When he was near appliances he was able to short circuit them, often burning out certain parts.

"He tried to communicate in this manner, but only succeeded in causing more havoc within the family. He did not agree to go into the *Light,* as it is called, until much later."

I saw that Quem was giving me more detail, resulting in more questions. "Quem, this past life that he had been a farmer…was this the first time he had done that sort of thing?"

"No, it was not the first time. However, now is not the best time to discuss any of that.

"My words are intended for teaching. I wish for the reader to know that people have propensities and these are for reason.

"After Bradley agreed to go into the higher realms with the angels he rested for quite some time. It was only after this time of complete rest that he was approached on the inner levels to take some classes to assist him in sorting out his choices. He completed his studies. Before incarnating again Bradley stated that he wanted to assist you in some manner. However, because of past momentums, his offer was rejected. We say he had intentions for the highest good, but had not achieved certain level of self-mastery in order to be granted this opportunity.

"Nakala! Your son, he is currently embodied and at the age of three years. We ask that you pray for him, dear one. Pray for his Divine guidance to give him patience, hope, and *peace.* His previous impulsive tendencies have already manifested themselves. We desire you pray for intervention if need be. It is *his* to work through, Nakala; yet we desire to give him as much support as we possibly can."

Looking back, I couldn't recall the number of times that the masters had worked with me on Bradley's suicide. However, I have noticed that each time, I had had the *opportunity* to work through another layer of trauma. I had succeeded in releasing a tremendous amount of pent-up emotion, most of which I had never realized that I carried in the first place. Fortunately, as time had gone on, the releases had been not as powerful or tiring. In other words, my heart hadn't hurt so much, the tears weren't so heavy, and it hadn't taken so long for me to recover from the ordeal.

Through each episode, Nathanal, my twin flame and my beloved, had tenderly coached me, "Nakala, be kind to yourself. Tonight, run yourself a salt bath complete with some fragrances; light a candle. Put on some soft music and drink some Chamomile tea. Be with it. This, what I suggest will aid in the releases. Take your time and enjoy this gift that you give to yourself; love yourself." This time had been no different.

Even though it had been twenty years since Bradley's passing, sometimes I still just wanted to let it all loose and cry. Instead, though, I chose to breathe deeply, expand my love, and be grateful for the time I had with him. For the first time, as I remembered some of the really good times, I felt myself smile.

"Nakala, dearest, take yourself some time and get some lunch. Come back to me in a while when you feel complete."

✳ ✳ ✳

When I came back to my desk, I felt refreshed and ready to get on with it. I had thought that maybe we would delve into another topic. Not so.

It seemed like Quem had an agenda concerning past momentums as he picked up where we had left off.

"Nakala, dearest, I spoke of people building momentums and carrying them forward into the next embodiment. This is true in other areas of your lives as well. I speak of your love of the arts and of writing! These ways of expression have carried over from previous lives, building and expanding: creating momentums. You came into this life exhibiting certain traits assisting you in defining areas of interest and guiding you in the attainment of skills necessary in completing your sacred contract or your soul's purpose on this journey. There have been other areas in your life that you have noticed to take a bit of extra effort and refinement in order to succeed.

"Also, I point out your desire to connect with your Divine Essence, the God in you, has been strong enough that you have been able to go forward and accomplish a veritable impetus on that count as well. You had built a strong momentum and carried these traits forward to your present incarnation. This is why you find it easier to do certain things and why you enjoy certain activities more than others.

"In short, you have become comfortable in these areas, receiving the spiritual gifts and integrating these skills or gifts in order for you to share them with others. These momentums were embedded into your cellular memory until the time has been correct to awaken them. You see now that you have developed and incorporated these gifts into the design of your life relatively easily.

"I do not wish to make my teaching sound elementary as this is certainly not the case: there are many levels to what I speak of and many circumstances that will project an influence on how you express yourself in any given life."

CHAPTER
TWENTY-TWO

"Nakala, earlier, I spoke to you of your biological brother, David. Now you understand he is your Pleiadian brother, as well. He, too, had passed prematurely of his own accord, by his own hand, Dear One: cause and effect.

"When I told you David was your Pleiadian brother, my son, you closed yourself down. Adamantly, you refused to hear my message to you of your connection with him. Your anger toward him hasn't subsided much in over fifteen years.

"We have seen a bit of progress. Slowly, you have been reaching a place of forgiveness for when, to your dismay, he took a handful of assorted drugs and stopped breathing, leaving behind a wife and four young children with no means of support. You have not come to terms with his action even though it happened nearly fifteen years ago.

"Nakala, look at this will you? David had a previous embodiment as an American Indian, Cherokee to be exact. He, alongside of his wife and daughter, (you) and many others Indians against their will had been extracted and held on reservations in Oklahoma Territory in the 1800's. The government had subsidized the Indians somewhat by giving them meat and flour (not always the best quality) to fortify their diets. During this same time Indians were also introduced to alcohol. Many of them became addicts. Your father had become an alcoholic, and he was a mean one at that. Your mother, who you also know this go-around (embodiment), was a spiritual woman and remained silent during his bouts of rage.

"To sum up your lifetime, your upbringing had been executed with an abusive father."

Quem stopped talking and suddenly projected a vision to me. In an instant, I saw a few beaded items near the blanket that I sat on. I had the sinew and the needle in my hand and several small gourd containers next to me with different colored beads.

Intuitively, I knew that I had used beading as a means for support: traded for food or sold for money. I knew that I had beaded whatever I could: moccasins, belts, and quivers to bring in some food. In addition, I had created beautiful woven baskets and containers made from gourds.

The vision stopped for a few moments; then suddenly he projected another scene. He knew I had received in fullness when I reacted to it by gasping out loud. I saw my father come into the tepee, grab a beautiful beaded man's belt, and take it with him. He didn't look my way. I knew that he aimed to trade it for whiskey. "The shame of it all," I had murmured.

"Your father had been robbed of his livelihood. But more importantly, his freedom had been stolen right before his very eyes. His defiance resulted in severe punishments: food had been withheld.

The chiefs and warriors were often considered as rebellious because their role had been to protect and provide. At first they argued, to no avail, with those who had been left in charge. It was a regular occurrence that those who had been disobedient were whipped and shot.

"Before the Cherokee Removal, as it is named, David had been a successful hunter for his family, providing well. The area of the reservation where they had been forced to live had been over-harvested of game to the point that the hunters came back empty-handed most of the time.

"Most of the men were broken, no longer able to express themselves—no longer did their words have merit. No longer were they able to provide provisions for their family or the tribe. As their custom, hunters went out in small groups to hunt and shared the harvest with those who were less fortunate (widows or the elders). Before the days of the reservation there had been great celebrations when the hunters came back with game. The entire community (tribe) went into celebration thanking Creator for their bounty! Now there were times few that warranted even a slight hint of joy.

"David had been a skillful warrior, Nakala, strong and true, who had been crippled by the white man's greed. The drink came to create a void, if you will, and to stupefy the senses! What good was he? Anger, resentment…hate ran deep. The longer he was forced to live in what he referred to as inhuman conditions, the more deeply ingrained his feelings became. Once he had been an honorable man who was deeply respected. Now? The drink served to temporarily lay at rest his feelings of inadequacy.

"The momentum to bury his anger with whiskey had been more than well-established and carried forward into the next embodiment when the two of you were siblings. Of course, with this next embodiment, evolution had taken its course: new methods were available to still the mind and the heart. However, the trauma from the previous life and the momentum created to still the trauma remained strong!

"After years of experimentation—that began in childhood, by the way—David discovered that his choice of self-medication was a variety of pills to ease his moments of discomfort. Pills served him in his time of need when it was too obvious or inappropriate to take the drink. Do you understand that the purpose of the drink or substance was to drown out—to subdue the feelings—to keep them at a manageable level?"

Quem did not wait for me to answer but continued with his teaching, "When the two of you were growing up, his hate and anger were constantly on the surface. Since you were younger, a girl, and left unattended on many occasions, he directed his unhappiness upon you."

"Seriously, Quem, *unhappiness?* That word is an understatement. Don't you think?"

"Ah, Nakala, let us not revisit that. You were readily available were you not? You remember that he exhibited strong tendencies of cruelty toward animals and anyone in his wake.

"Unfortunately, David did not have proper counseling for him to work through his feelings during childhood. At that time the knowledge of past lives was unheard of."

My heart grew heavy as I listened to Quem's account. "Quem," I said, "what you say makes me feel so sad for him and ashamed that I…I don't want to write this but it is true. I hated him. He was beyond cruel and wouldn't listen to anything our parents told him.

"The entire time, I had attributed his behavior to his being adopted. All during my childhood I thought he was jealous of me. I had never been able to understand why he hated me so much."

Still, Quem did not address my questions. Instead, he continued on with his narrative, "So you see, Nakala, Bradley and David had similar accounts. The interesting thing here, you see, is you all have stories…areas that you work to suppress. Nakala, you do as well."

I nodded my head and replied, "Nice. I wondered when you would get around to me. I know well, Quem, that I have *issues* in certain areas but"…my voice trailed off. "What exactly are you saying here?"

"I am saying that you have suppressed feelings of unworthiness just like Bradley and David did. The difference is the severity of the suppression. Perhaps I put it this way? The difference is how deeply you have allowed yourself to become entrenched in the muck and mire of it all.

"You have been working on releasing embedded beliefs that do not serve you since shortly after Bradley's passing. I'd say on a conscious level you have been letting go of anger and so on for fifteen years and working to re-establish a healthier spiritual view of life overall. As time continues, you become more efficient at the task, allowing you to release great measures of darkness from your bodies all. I am referring to the four lower bodies: mental, emotional, spiritual (etheric), and physical.

"You are a matrix of energies—a Divine Cosmic Matrix. Ah, you know not the complexity of which I speak. Rest assured we will get into a more in depth teaching at a later time."

PART
SEVEN

THE PLEIADIAN
COUNCIL OF LIGHT

CHAPTER
TWENTY-THREE

Over the years, many beings have come to speak to me. I have found that certain guides, masters, and angels specialize in different areas or tasks. Below is a list of some of the areas that I have experienced their assistance in.

* Radiating healing energy: some have told me that they are radiating energy; others remain silent.

* Shown love and compassion through the guidance, healing, and teachings.

* Some have merely introduced themselves—say hello and verbally offer nothing else to me.

* Guides have channeled through me pictures, the Pleiadian written word, and what I call their sign language.

* Some have given personal guidance (like assist me by picking out what clothes to wear or purchase or what to buy or what and how to prepare meals). This may seem odd but everything has a vibration; and clothing and food may influence our thoughts and emotions, resulting in a higher, the same, or a lower vibration.

* Assisting me to perfectly rephrase or reformulate my thoughts (be it on paper or in conversation): e.g. affirmations and

calls to the I AM Presence (the God in me) and to correctly ask questions to the masters and other beings of the higher realms, resulting in an answer that will truly benefit myself and or others.

* While traveling I receive guidance on which route to take, which hotels and restaurants to use. (They do this in response to my asking them for assistance in that specific area.)

* I have been constantly observed or studied: e.g. my thoughts, feelings, behaviors. Some will let you know they are doing this; others will not. One reason, I have been told, is this is their way to plan strategically the best way to teach me.

* The masters will often teach other guides while working with me, using my life experiences. (Contrary to belief, guides do not instantly know how to guide. There are certain rules and techniques they must learn and follow.)

* There are a multitude of organizations, committees, and councils that work on my behalf to bring information to help me throughout my evolution (to assist me in awakening to my true God-Self).

* I have seen Beings of Light appear before me and images of beings projected to me.

* The longer I have taken dictation from them, the more expanded and detailed the information has become. Meaning, they work with me as I am ready to receive.

The above information is to give you a rough overview of what ascended masters, angels, and guides do to assist us. We must remember that there are boundaries—we have free will and this will affect what the guides may or may not do in, through, and around us.

In addition, there are the three A's. Ask for what you desire, Allow it to come to you (in a way you may not expect or even recognize), and Accept the gifts with gratitude.

There are universal laws that the Beings of Light must honor.

CHAPTER
TWENTY-FOUR

Before my move from Paola, Kansas, one evening I had been sitting in mediation when I heard the ascended master Samuel Paul announce, "Nakala, prepare yourself for some guests tomorrow, Sunday morning at 9:00."

This instruction, in itself, wasn't all that unusual, but for some reason, this time, I felt a little uneasy with his particular directive. Samuel Paul didn't elaborate on the matter and I didn't ask for any more detail concerning it. I let it pass.

Over the years I have learned to accept the information he gives me. As I said, though, this time the statement made me feel a bit uncomfortable. Looking closer at my feelings, I ascertained that the difference with this directive was that I had been given a specific date and time. How Samuel Paul had chosen to give me the news sounded more formal as if he were introducing someone of great significance. I couldn't be sure though. I felt that the *way* he had announced the date indicated something out of the ordinary was about to occur. Maybe, I surmised, I was about to get some new guides or perhaps I would be told to change directions concerning my book or even they might tell me that they wanted me to go somewhere. I felt that being given a certain time was a telltale sign there were beings of high standing going to arrive. Nevertheless, I never knew for sure what Samuel Paul planned.

It was fortunate that the day and time that had been selected was perfect because it was one of my days off from writing.

The morning came and I had been meditating while I waited for the guests to arrive. The first thing I heard was, "It is time to begin. We will be creating a new journal." I went to the closet to where my stash was located and began to reach for the stack of blank journals when I heard, "There, the pink one, that will work. Get that one." I noted that the book was neon pink. *What an interesting choice. Who were these guys?*

I knew that this signified the beings or people planned to meet with me again. However, even with getting a new journal, it was a never a sure thing as there had been many times that I had prepared a new journal with someone who had requested it and they had given me only one transmission. I simply had labeled it, placed it on shelf in alphabetical order and gone on.

I opened the pink journal and wrote down the location, day, and time of the transmission all the while expecting to hear someone different speak—someone that I had not met before. However, it was Quem who spoke. *Weird!*

Quem began with, "We come together today in reverence to Our Father-Our Creator who reigns over all in the name of The Christ. Amen."

I didn't understand why Quem would be speaking as all of his dictations go into my personal journal.

Quem continued on, "We see much has been accomplished in this home and we are pleased to give forth the release of your presence here [Paola, Kansas] as your contract has been satisfied. (This brought up another subject: I had not realized that I had had a contract here.)

"The energies that bubble up of sadness and grief are to release you from your past ties to these peoples—your energetic qualifications, your endeavors—as it is time for you to move on to another experience. All is well.

"These feeling energies are to be expected and you are to relax in the knowing as they are to assist you to move forward. You are letting go of energies unwanted and unneeded; they have bound you and controlled you. All energies that are not of the Light are to be transmuted into *Light!* Call upon Saint Germain's Legions of Violet Ray Angels of Freedom and Transmutation to assist you in this task!

"Dear daughter, Nakala, all is well within the Realms of Light—those who watch over you—assisting you throughout your walk on this plane.

"You are heavy-burdened with several works. It is time to complete and let go of the energy. Finish the first book in the series of *The Accounts of a Pleiadian Traveler.* (Quem's reference was to this book.) It is a joy to see you love the work as you do.

"Remember, my Love, all works serve particular and we give unto you these works for the highest good.

"We are many. I am your father, Quem. I am a member of this council. Tora Tee holds the head seat of this council—*The Pleiadian Council of Light!*"

The way Quem stated, *The Pleiadian Council of Light,* I intuitively knew that this council was one of the highest stations in the Pleiadian Nation and the cosmos. Whatever *The Pleiadian Council of Light's* intentions, connections, and goals were, they were extremely important to our evolution—our ascension! The reverence I felt was palpable.

Quem then reminded me, "Tora Tee came to you a few days past. He is ready to see you in your rightful place, as we all are!" (No one had ever made it clear what was meant by my 'rightful place'. It could have been my next place of residence, back home in Myra, Pleiades, or to have completed my ascension to the fifth dimensional level of consciousness.)

Then Quem did a quick but in-depth overview of upcoming commitments that I was to take care of in the next few days and weeks.

After he seemed to be satisfied with his summary, Quem promptly told me to get my recorder out as the meeting was about to begin. He desired that I record the dictation. I did as he requested.

The meeting was then handed over to someone who identified himself as Joshua. There was no mistaking that the speaker was of high standing.

These guys were into some critical work. I knew it. Why then did they want to meet with me? Why would they want to give me a transmission? I guess at first I thought I didn't measure up to receive this type of communication.

On the physical level, preparing for my first meeting with *The Pleiadian Council of Light* or *PCL* really wasn't any different than taking dictation from one of the archangels or masters or channeling a spiritual reading for a client. However, for me, it *felt* different. Just the name indicated an organization that held the position of a higher level of Light and a whole lot of responsibility. They trusted me somehow as it was plain that they had taken me into their confidence.

Before our meeting, I had lit a white candle that sat on the coffee table and made the call to honor these Beings of Light: that I would receive what was for the highest good. I affirmed that I am a representative of the Pleiadian Nation and always I allow the messages to come through me perfectly, affirming that my choice was to serve to the best of my ability. I had put some meditative music on, turning the volume down so it soothed me but didn't distract me from the communication. Before I sat down to receive, I *always* had my house tidied up (papers filed, dishes washed, bed made) and was always fully dressed as if I were having someone coming to visit me.

It isn't like I have to open the door for them when they arrive or must prepare seating for them although they welcome this offering. I do not see them like I would see someone in the physical. However, they see me.

There are times that I can sense them, or an image is projected into my mind showing me who is there and what they look like. The details, to date, are usually not crystal-clear but I do get an idea where they stand or sit, what type of dress they wear, their hair color and style and so on. In other words, I am mindful that I have guests; and I want them to be comfortable in my home.

I have to laugh because when I go to a restaurant and sit at a booth, I (by habit) have always sat (usually still do) in the middle of the bench. Since I have been consciously aware that Nathanal travels with me he will invariably say, "Nakala, move over will you?" That in itself makes me think they, at least sometimes, like to sit down and that our chairs serve them just fine.

Joshua touched on various topics, one being the name of this particular sector of the council. He said that this group represented Earth Commissions. He projected an image that radiated Light: a hub with several spokes extending outward forming another circle. It looked similar to a wagon wheel to me; only it had a soft golden glow. The hub represented *The Pleiadian Council of Light* and each shaft represented a group or committee designated to oversee certain projects. Comterous is one of the committees and the group who had been working with me from the beginning. However, I had not understood that they were affiliated with any council. In truth there are many hubs and many spokes, all pointing outward or downward into the outer or lowest realm: Earth.

The Comterous is one group who directly inspires and directs people to fulfill their soul's contract by using the media to reach the mainstream or collective consciousness concerning subjects like spirit or the unseen and the metaphysical.

Imagine, if you will, each subject matter has a specific committee with a sizable membership to inspire, guide, and direct our progress: music, horticulture, science, astronomy, physics, oceanography, modes of transportation, the arts, and so on. There are beings on the inner levels or higher realms of Light who oversee all of this: Beings who inspire us, give us ideas and so on. (The reason for this is that we have moved *away* or *separated* from our I AM Presence (our God-Selves.)) At present the masters are our mediators giving us messages from our I AM Presence until we can once again join with It and listen to Its promptings and direct guidance.

After Joshua explained the basic workings of committees like Comterous and had lightly touched on my physical move to be near my parents, he said, "We have specific intent to our work. We speak on your work as our scribe. You bring down our messages, the dictations, anchoring them into the energy of the sphere of Earth to join with like energy. This makes stronger our purpose—our design.

"You are entering a new phase—new journey—new contract. As of this moment you do not know your true purpose of this new contract we speak of.

"You, Nakala, will continue your channeling, writing, and teaching. But, we say, in addition, there is more. You are to bring forth the Lemurian teachings to the forefront. There have been others who began this work. You are to continue. Do not misunderstand: it takes many to establish. You are but one." (Joshua was talking about the continent of Lemuria that had sunk thousands of years ago. What remained was a colony that had been established underground—specifically inside the mountain called Shasta in Northern California. The High Priest, Adama, has been one of the beings who took on the task of educating the residents of the outer level of Earth on behalf of their community, Telos.)

Joshua continued, "You are to work with *many!* You began long ago, Miss. It is time to work again in this area. We are always with you. Always! Nakala, we will meet again this coming Sunday at 9:00 AM. Please be punctual." Joshua then signed off by saying, "We Are One!"

With Joshua's words I began to speculate. Letting the words roll over my tongue again and again. *Did he mean that I would take dictation from Adama or possibly others who reside in Telos? What did he really mean?*

✳ ✳ ✳

As promised, the second meeting began at precisely 9:00 AM the following Sunday morning. Babaró who is my guardian and works with me on the writings began with, "The flame of Illumination is greatly amplified this day. We are sending our thoughts and prayers that this great yellow flame is amplified, easily felt, seen, and heard over the entire plant. All is being illumined: such beauty to behold! Tiger Eye and Topaz are the stones that support the Illumination Flame.

"Nakala, we thank you for preparing the home for the council's meeting. The energies here, they are peaceful.

"To begin with, for your benefit, Nakala, we will announce the presence of all who are in attendance today: Quem, Sarah, Nathanal, Suzette, Samuel Paul, Sakeem, Jonson, Tabitha, Camilla, Tulró, Ahseem, Napoleon, Christian, I, and others who are viewing remotely." (I made a mental note that some of the people Babaró had named I had never heard of.)

To acknowledge my thought Babaró stated, "New names, new faces: not all are members of this council. However, we have invited many, as these people are amplifying our intentions that are created anew and those intentions that are held at this moment.

"We have special for you, Nakala on this day. You are Princess of Myra, the Kingdom of the Akasie in the star system of the Pleiades. Princess Nakala…." (In my mind's eye I saw all bow before me.)

Immediately I was overcome with emotion at being addressed like this. Because I was seated, I put my hands together in a prayerful mudra and did a half bow in return as I said, "Thank you, Thank you."

"Nakala, you have not seen yourself in this light although you have been privy to this information. Because of the type of life you lead in the physical realm, you may agree that you lead a rather average existence. But look to yourself, Nakala; you are nothing of the sort...average? This word, average gave you comfort moments ago as you were not singled out. But know Dear Heart, you are unique, exceptional, presenting yourself as such. You wonder why you rise above some of your peers, offering yourself in the best light possible. You surround yourself with beauty. Your life, as well as your home, must be organized. It is because of your superior upbringing—your position in the hierarchy of the Akasie! Rest assured you have a great momentum on this count because of your Divine Inheritance!

"This is truly who you are. We bow to you and honor you as it has taken a tremendous amount of courage to give yourself over to work in this realm. Indeed a sacrifice. You, like us, could be enjoying the luxuries of Myra right now. Instead, we must strategically plot our next move to assist those who reside here on Earth in the physical form. I speak not only of the humans but also of the animal and nature kingdoms as well, as these, in addition, must be emancipated from the dense energies. All must go into the beautiful Light as we have.

"Now we get on with it. The reason for our meeting is to plan our next step to bringing this project—the books—all to the hands of the readers. We came together this morning to share with you that all in attendance are amplifying the intention and holding that amplification of intention that the books are written perfectly, timely, and then dispensed to the masses accordingly for the higher good All!

"We know this project is dear to your heart and we know that because you reside in the physicality, forgetting the ways of the Masters of Light, you require push—guidance in order to continue forth. Always know we are behind you, supporting this endeavor.

"*The Pleiadian Council of Light* is involved in many projects. This one, yours, is but one. Nevertheless, it gets our attention full!

"You are one of the trusted and valued scribes for the Pleiadian Nation. We thank you.

"Because you believe with your heart this is your true path—God's design for you—beauty, abundance, grace, the writings all continue to flow to...through you easily like the bubbling brook waters flow effortlessly.

"We say, just now, do not become too comfortable as we must continue to go forth taking you into territories unknown to expand awareness—consciousness—and raising your vibration. The goal here is to reach full momentum, attaining the fifth dimensional level of consciousness.

"We back you 100% to bring forth the teachings from the Lemurians to assist humanity. The city of Telos holds valuable sacred teachings that are to be shared. You will be connected with those who will bring forth all."

"Wait, just a minute here." I said, "Lemurians? I understand that they held or hold as you say sacred teachings. But what do I have to do with them? What do you have to do with them?"

"Nakala, dear one, there are nations or peoples many who have gathered here for the purpose of raising you up (you personally and the masses). The Telosians are but one group. There are many Pleiadians who have joined with those who reside in Telos. The people of Telos work with those who are of the Light. They have valuable insight to offer as you venture forward, taking you into the Light. We are united as One. They offer their hand to us and in turn to you. You see?

"You know, Dear One, these people are your people as you have lived among them for many years. For now I lay down this subject. In time, Nakala, all is to be revealed.

"The message here is you have our full support and attention. You will continue on like you have—only you are to connect with our energy: INVINCIBLE! There is no stopping us!

"Yes, you have free-will and should you desire to remove self for any reason, we will not hold you. However, we know your honor, loyalty, discipline, and most of all your love for the peoples.

"It is time we close for the day. It is important to gather like this each week—regroup—reset our intentions. We are pleased to have these moments. ~We Are One~

✳ ✳ ✳

Again, it was stated to me that we would meet the following Sunday.

This time I had completed all of my tasks and had sat down at 8:45 AM when, without delay, I heard someone announce that since we were all ready, we would begin.

This was the third meeting and I had begun to feel more relaxed with the process. I was developing a discipline—a habit—yet was learning to be flexible.

The meeting began with, "We are One. We begin today in remembrance of all those who came before us to illumine our path so we may tread in Light instead of darkness.

"Masters you all are! The lives you have lived together? Know in this level your memory sleeps." (This was in reference to some people I had been directed to meet with the previous evening.)

"You felt that you resonated with those in attendance like you had known them from long ago. In truth you were nearly all at the same level of awareness and vibration. All had been summoned to join as one in amplifying radiation for purpose to you unknown.

"There were no airs put on. All was, as you put it, 'Real!'

"We were there in attendance as other representatives of various councils were, as well. The rooms were overflowing!

"You ask my name. Jordan. I am council advisor. We work together to bring certain who have taken embodiment in order to shift out of the old and into the new." (I noticed that Jordan had a different way of speaking and wanted to make sure that none of his meaning was lost in transcription.)

"This is your reality and you must create anew. This is but one universal law. We assist gladly!

"The group of thirteen is your committee [Comterous] and you have entwined yourself with the energies of this group creating One!

"Make no mistake of what we say here and now. The people [of the group] mean business and you have already begun the shift. Continue on!

"Now concerning the books written by the Comterous. You are being given special.

"Samuel Paul has received the next manuscript to be presented to you. The other is to be disregarded. You begin tomorrow. It…the transmission will go quickly and for you bring excitement and confidence that is required in order to carry endeavor forward. (I had been working to rewrite a manuscript and this was to be discarded.)

"The book you previously worked on, *In the Light of Day: Book Three* of this series was used for healing on a particular level. We will use this book. Be it known that some of same concepts will be used in another book. You will soon write the conclusion to bring readers into alignment with following volume [in the series].

"All five books have been completed and will be handed off to you quickly, Nakala. No more delays.

Quickly Jordan spoke as if he had an outline that he followed, "We began the meeting early. Learning to be flexible is of noble value and should be allowed with all meetings and communications. What we do here takes precedence over all other endeavors. Balance is your key to going forward."

✳ ✳ ✳

After I had typed out the recorded dictations from the *Pleiadian Council of Light* meetings, Babaró explained, "We have specifically asked you to include these dictations in this book, *Awakenings: The Gift*, for purpose to teach those who reside on the outer levels of consciousness that there is architecture or structure to the goings on in the Higher Realms. There are a multitude of beings who are stationed in your aerospace and on the Earth herself to make themselves available to those who have arrived at the specific level of consciousness desirous of a higher understanding.

"We have chosen a different sequence in teaching you about councils, committees, and subcommittees and how they are individual yet they form a broader or larger, further developed, anatomy of hierarchy."

✳ ✳ ✳

Three weeks had gone by with three consecutive meetings. It was plain for me to conclude that it was Comterous of Earth Commissions, which is a sub-committee of *The Pleiadian Council of Light* who were actually holding the meetings. To me, it seemed strange that they had not ever revealed to me anything about the head council and why many of the dictations in the meetings had dealt with my own personal issues and the work that I do as a Channel of Light.

Speaking in a tender manner, Babaró said, "Nakala, our aim is not to leave you unattended (not address your personal concerns). We discuss your individual issues because you are expanding on the lower level of consciousness and joining with the Christ Consciousness. You are learning to work directly with the Presence, the I AM, which is the God in you, by setting your ego in line. Because you are in the ascension program, the masters are teaching you how to let go—transmute—and create positive energy all in a focused manner. There is much more to this, so much more. Know that we are using this opportunity—to serve to direct you home.

"You and many others who are Pleiadians wanted to live on this Earth in a lower dimension to have the experience of having a physical body, physical things, and physical senses. This was an experiment of sorts and something that I suppose you could say intrigued you—gave you reason for being. Some have been here for eons, having been caught in the cycles of life and death. You, Nakala, are one who came to assist the people as they awakened (remembered) to the gift of their Divine essence. This is truly the reason you came to experience the physical.

"When you became aware that you are not alone, that you have Divine assistance, guidance, love, and protection from us, you began to understand and you must go through the awakening process. Many of you receive "gifts" which are psychic advancements to further your understanding of how all of us are connected. The gifts are part of the awakening.

"Nakala, Love flows unto you from the Cosmic Void through us back out of you to the Cosmic Void creating a full circle. This love is power-energy. Electricity is your term for this power.

"This is important for you to know: energy is magnetic and if it is not intentionally directed will go to where it matches in frequency.

"There are levels or what we call octaves of energy each radiating its own specific frequency. You are the creator of, and you are creating with, this energy by your intention through your very own thoughts, emotions, and actions.

"Energy travels by the way of sacred geometry—the three dimensional symmetrical shapes that humans use as building blocks for architecture and design.

"What is given to you by the way of the Cosmic Void is your Divine Inheritance. As a Divine Cosmic Being you are to use this energy that is gifted to you and used accordingly for the Will of God, for good! Do you see how powerful you are? Energy is cycled continually to all life forms and intelligences because all are part of the God—all are God."

CONCLUSION

Awakening: The Gift has been truly a pleasure to write. Through the years I have discovered a great deal about myself with the assistance of the Masters of Light. I look back in amazement…in total wonder, at specific events in my life. Even though some have been horrific, everything I have experienced has assisted me in finding my path—my place in this world—the place that I know is rightfully mine.

I am a traveler from far away—the Pleiades: a star nation populated by a great number of souls who agreed to lead those who reside on this Earth through times of tremendous upheaval and of great transcendence: the Awakening of our Divinity.

As I learn to express my Divinity through a body of flesh, I go through trials that literally stop me in my tracks, I wonder if I have learned the lesson well enough or even if I am understanding them. I know if I don't integrate my lessons correctly I will receive the same lessons again and again until I do. I wonder how the lessons will appear the next time. There is no way I can know what the future will present; only that I am here to do the best that I can.

It is through the writings—these books—that the Masters of Light give to you their wisdom. The teachings are universal and timeless. "Breathe easy," the Masters say. "Learn to live with true abandon by loving with all of your heart. Do what makes your heart sing."

Love,
Nakala

ACKNOWLEDGEMENTS

I'd like to offer my sincere gratitude to JoyAn Tucker
for her friendship and editing expertise and to
Raymond Fuller, my soul mate and best friend, who
was instrumental in seeing this book to completion.